KT-431-390

C

3 0 JUN 2017

Books should be returne
date above. Renew by pi
online *www.kent.gov.uk/l*

CUSTOMER
SERVICE
EXCELLENCE

CSE

Ke
Cou
Cou
kent.go

Libraries Registration & Archives

C161032990

The Cowboy SEAL's Jingle Bell Baby

LAURA MARIE ALTOM

All rights reserved including the right of reproduction in whole or in part in any form. This edition is published by arrangement with Harlequin Books S.A.

This is a work of fiction. Names, characters, places, locations and incidents are purely fictional and bear no relationship to any real life individuals, living or dead, or to any actual places, business establishments, locations, events or incidents. Any resemblance is entirely coincidental.

This book is sold subject to the condition that it shall not, by way of trade or otherwise, be lent, resold, hired out or otherwise circulated without the prior consent of the publisher in any form of binding or cover other than that in which it is published and without a similar condition including this condition being imposed on the subsequent purchaser.

® and TM are trademarks owned and used by the trademark owner and/or its licensee. Trademarks marked with ® are registered with the United Kingdom Patent Office and/or the Office for Harmonisation in the Internal Market and in other countries.

First Published in Great Britain 2016
By Mills & Boon, an imprint of HarperCollins*Publishers*
1 London Bridge Street, London, SE1 9GF

Large Print edition 2017

© 2016 Laura Marie Altom

ISBN: 978-0-263-07175-7

Our policy is to use papers that are natural, renewable and recyclable products and made from wood grown in sustainable forests. The logging and manufacturing processes conform to the legal environmental regulations of the country of origin.

Printed and bound in Great Britain
by CPI Antony Rowe, Chippenham, Wiltshire

Laura Marie Altom is a bestselling and award-winning author who has penned nearly fifty books. After college (go, Hogs!), Laura Marie did a brief stint as an interior designer before becoming a stay-at-home mom to boy-girl twins and a bonus son. Always an avid romance reader, she knew it was time to try her hand at writing when she found herself replotting the afternoon soaps.

When not immersed in her next story, Laura plays video games, tackles Mount Laundry and, of course, reads romance!

Laura loves hearing from readers at either PO Box 2074, Tulsa, OK 74101, or by email, balipalm@aol.com.

Love winning fun stuff? Check out lauramariealtom.com.

When I asked my daughter who this book should be dedicated to, she smiled and said, "Duh—me and Yeti." Yeti's her big, doofus black Lab who's so naughty that he actually takes time away from my writing. He doesn't in any way deserve a book dedication, but since he's so cute, I'll cave… :-)

For Hannah & Yeti

Prologue

'Twas the night before Easter...

"How about letting a cowboy buy you a drink?" Navy SEAL Rowdy Jones slurred his words, but the evening's libations bolstered his courage. As such, he'd moseyed over to the gorgeous little hottie who'd stolen his last rational thought.

She appraised him as if he were a stud sire up for auction.

"Want me to spin around so you get the full

force of my magnetic attraction?" he asked with a grin.

In a dive bar filled with boot-wearing, beer-guzzling cowboys, she sipped a martini. Her white dress clung tight enough to have been painted on. She had the face of an angel, with cherry-red lips and a sleek wave of blond hair his fingertips knew would feel silky.

Instead of speaking, she downed more of her drink, then raised her hand, motioning for him to twirl.

More than a little turned on by her silent take-charge demeanor, he raised his longneck beer high, gyrating his ass in time with George Strait's "All My Ex's Live in Texas."

He didn't just want this gal; he *had* to have her—all of her. Down and dirty and every way in between.

In his thirty-odd years, he'd gotten pretty good at sizing up a man's or woman's character. The woman's exterior screamed iceberg dead ahead. But a sadness in her eyes made him wonder if her carefully applied outer persona was eggshell fragile.

"Like what you see?" he asked on the turn around.

Without a trace of a smile, she nodded.

"Wanna get a room?"

She nodded again.

She set her drink on the bar, then held out her hand as if she were a princess and he her loyal subject.

His brain couldn't quite compute the fact that she was taking him up on his offer, but he wasn't complaining. He paid their bar tabs, then led her through the maze of Saturday-night heroes, all striving to outshine one another with their tall tales.

Though the next morning would ring in Easter, their miserable portion of North Dakota hadn't gotten the memo. Earlier that night at the annual rodeo, the temperature had been pleasant enough, but a front must've moved in and cold wind whipped his mystery gal's formerly smooth hair into a wild, sexy tangle.

Given the nasty weather, the bar's exterior was lonely. Neon beer signs glowed through dusty windows. The parking lot's one light didn't do much to show their way to the adjoining motel.

Giddy Up Inn wasn't fancy, but he'd heard from temporary cowboys hired to move cattle from seasonal ranges that it was clean.

The lobby was plain.

A single red Formica counter held a cash register and a few struggling plants. The air smelled of Lysol and the coffee brewing on a corner stand.

Rowdy paid cash for the room, and the weary-looking clerk handed over an actual key attached to a plastic horseshoe.

Back outside, Rowdy sheltered his dream girl

from the worst of the wind. He found room twenty-one and slipped the key into the lock.

The room was cold, so he quickly shut the door and turned on the heat.

The woman stood just inside the door.

She hugged herself and looked on the verge of crying.

"Look," he said, "if you'd rather call this off, I'd understand." He hooked his thumbs in his Wranglers' back pockets. "I mean, I'd be lying if I said I wouldn't be disappointed, but my momma raised me to be a gentleman and—"

"You always talk this much?"

She flew at him like a summer wind—wild and hot.

She braced her hands to his stubbled cheeks, slanting her lips across his with what he could describe only as an angry, frenzied need. He met the sweep of her tongue and groaned.

When she reached for his belt buckle, he was all too happy to help her along. She jerked his denim shirt open with enough force to rain buttons onto the carpeted floor. She pressed her small, nimble hands to his chest, kneading his pecs, skimming his abs. She trailed her lips over his bare skin, nipping his left biceps, sucking the hollow at the base of his neck.

Her every action screamed desperation.

The gentleman in him wondered why.

The horny bastard only wanted more.

He spun her around, jerking down the zipper on her dress. It might be white, but her attitude was bad-girl red. He let the garment drop to the floor, and with her back to him, he kissed her neck, cupping his hand to her belly to press her against his obvious need.

Her bra and panties weren't from around these parts. White lace fine enough for him to rip off her with his teeth yet fancy to the degree he wasn't ashamed to admit he felt damn near intimidated.

As if her curves weren't tough enough to

handle, there was her scent—once again at odds with her outer ice queen. How could she look so cold, and yet, when he breathed her in, smell like sunshine and lemonade or wild-flowers swaying in a gentle breeze.

His physical ache to be inside her had grown to a near-frantic need. A nagging voice told him to at least dig a condom from his wallet. After a few tries in between kisses, he finally managed to roll one on. But too many beers and two hands filled with her ample breasts made him not much interested in anything beyond unlatching her bra and then dragging down the sheer panties.

She dropped his jeans and he was damned glad to have gone commando.

They were kissing again, and he found her hot and ready. Without thinking, he hefted her onto the dresser, then rammed all the way home. She cried out but then dug her fingers into his back, urging him faster and harder.

He didn't know her name or job or where she could possibly be from, but none of that mattered. She was his every wicked fantasy. His whole world encapsulated in a lemonade-scented dream.

He thrust until he couldn't think or breathe.

Until raw sensation struck him temporarily blind.

Mere moments after spilling his seed, he had to have her again…

Chapter One

'Twas almost the night before Halloween...

"Just shoot me..." Rowdy stared at his cell phone as if it had bit him.

"What's wrong?" His roommate and fellow navy SEAL, Logan, slurped from his milkshake.

"What do you think?" He glared at his friend, who was a genius with plastic explosives but apparently couldn't manage setting up autopay for their damn utility bills. "Try dropping your cell down an Afghanistan well, then slogging through six months' worth of voice mail. I'd delete it all but turns out some of this crap is important—like when the gas company calls with a recorded message explaining our service got turned off for nonpayment."

"Oops. Yeah, I meant to look into that. No wonder we've been stuck with cold showers." Logan shrugged and took another sip.

Rowdy rolled his eyes and moved on to the next message.

While his friends worked their way around Virginia Beach's Lynnhaven Mall's food court, sampling all the fast food they'd missed while overseas, Rowdy had been trapped at his cell phone provider's store, buying a new phone. He'd bummed Logan's for occasional chats with his parents, but since he'd been with the only other people he ever called, he figured there was no point in replacing it till now.

Just as Rowdy played the last message, Logan

signaled that he was headed to the Corn Dog Factory.

Paul Jameson—nicknamed Duck on account of his giant paddle feet—stood in line at Sbarro.

"Um, hello?" a woman said in a tentative tone. "Hope I have the right man? I'm trying to reach Rowdy? Gosh, I'm sorry. I just realized that though you gave me this number, I don't even know your last name. You might not remember me, but we shared a, um… Let's just say we were together—the night before Easter, and… I don't know any easy way to say this, so here goes. I'm pregnant. You're the father. But no worries—I'm putting the baby up for adoption, so you're off the hook. I already found an amazing family, and our son is g-going to lead a g-great life." Wait, what? *His son?* Her voice broke up. Was she crying? "Anyway, if I don't hear back from you soon, I'll assume this plan works for you, too. Bye." Click.

Stunned, Rowdy stood in the food court's center for what felt like an eternity while throngs of shoppers walked around him. How could an accidental pregnancy happen to him *twice*?

"Dude…" Logan slapped him on the back. "You look like hell. I didn't forget any other payments, did I?"

Rowdy stumbled into the nearest chair at the nearest table, then cued up the message again on his phone. "Listen."

Duck wandered up with a slice of pepperoni that was almost as big as his feet. He leaned in.

Logan sat, setting his corn-dog tray with about eighteen mustard packets in front of him. By the time the message had ended, he'd paled, too. "Dude… What the hell? Didn't you learn back in high school to always wear a raincoat?"

"I always do—did. This has to be another mistake." His mind flashed on that one brief doubt he'd had about his condom before plunging inside the woman who'd made him care about nothing other than giving her as much pleasure as she was giving him. Was it possible the condom broke?

"Then this chick must be like the other one who tried scamming you?"

"Exactly." Only that time, Logan knew for a fact his protection had been fully in force.

Duck said, "No wonder Ginny never lets me off my leash to play with you. Rowdy, you're a freakin' mess."

Rowdy glared at his supposed friend. The guy was married with four kids. His leash was a choke chain with links made of emotional steel. Poor guy hardly got out at all. But he seemed happy. Aside from their SEAL team, Duck's wife and kids were his world.

As for Rowdy? Being a SEAL was his world.

Period. End of story. But what if this woman was telling the truth…

He winced.

"When did she call?" Logan asked.

"Six months ago."

"Damn. So, like, your bun's almost ready to pop out of the oven?" Logan bit into his first of three corn dogs.

Rowdy pressed the heels of his hands to his throbbing forehead. "What am I going to do? Because one thing's for sure—there's no way in hell she's giving away my son. On the flip side, I'll be the first to admit I'm not marriage material."

"Great attitude, man." Duck smacked the back of Rowdy's head. He'd have considered popping him back, but Duck outweighed him by fifty pounds of pure muscle. "Get your head out of your ass and get a clue. Family life is great. You, me, Ginny and your new bride can all have cookouts on the beach. My kids will love playing with yours."

"See?" Logan stole a pepperoni from Duck's slice. "No worries. Already, we've downgraded this situation from a DEFCON 2 paternity emergency down to a nice, steady DEFCON 5 beach barbecue. We've got your back. Plus, I'll make a great uncle."

Some days Rowdy wished he had better friends.

EX-RODEO QUEEN, EX-WIFE and ex-debutante Tiffany Lawson was seven months pregnant and determined to squeeze her formerly size-six feet into a pair of her favorite Jimmy Choos. It was a given no clothes in her closet fit, but now her shoes wouldn't, either?

As for the no-good, rotten dirt clod of a cowboy who'd landed her in this position and hadn't even had the decency to call? He could go straight to Hades for all she cared. Rowdy was low-life pond scum—*lower*. She didn't even know his last name! Which, granted, didn't say a heckuva lot about her decision-making skills, but still…

The less time spent dwelling on him, the better.

"Honey, no matter how hard you try cramming your toes into those darlings, they're not going to fit." Her mother, former Dallas society maven Gigi Hastings-Lawson, didn't even bother looking up from the same copy of *Town & Country* she'd been reading for three months. Thanks to Big Daddy Lawson's slight issues with the law, she couldn't afford a new one. Since he'd be away for a nice long while and their Dallas mansion had been seized, Tiffany and her mother now lived in the godforsaken speck on the map known as Maple Springs, North Dakota.

Making matters worse—if that were even possible—was the fact that Tiffany didn't earn enough money in real estate to have her own place. She and her mom lived with her paternal grandmother, Pearl. Since Big Daddy had paid off her house long before his trouble with the law, authorities allowed her to keep it.

"You did hear it's supposed to snow?" Her mother lounged on the white velvet chaise Tiffany had salvaged from their former home by strapping it to the roof of the secondhand red Jeep Cherokee she'd bought from their former housekeeper.

Mr. Bojangles—her spoiled teacup Chihuahua—slept on her mother's lap. He wore a black sweater and rhinestone collar. It had become her own special ironic hell that her dog now dressed better than her.

"When is it not supposed to snow?" Tiffany peered out her bedroom window to find another gloomy day in her equally gloomy life.

Blustery wind shook Pearl's century-old home like a dog with a bone.

For comfort, she cupped her hands to her baby bump, but even that wasn't satisfying, knowing she'd soon give her son to the Parkers. They were an amazing couple—both attorneys. Jeb Parker was considering a gubernatorial campaign. Susie Parker promised as soon as the baby was born, she'd resign to stay home with their new son.

In her former life, Tiffany had much the same plans, but then her father's legal woes had been too much for her ex, Crawford, to deal with, and that had been that. He'd filed for a quiet divorce and was now married to one of her best friends—a former Miss Texas. *C'est la vie.*

Tiffany did learn one valuable lesson from her pain—men were as flighty as trash in the wind. Never to be trusted. They made you love them and then broke your heart. Okay, maybe that was more than one lesson, but bottom line, she would never, ever, *ever* give her heart to another man.

A twinge of guilt for her infant son made her hug her tummy. *You're excluded, little fella. You'll be the one man on the planet who's perfect in every way. I might not be physically with you while you're growing up, but I'll be with you every day in spirit.*

Tiffany reached for her hot-pink sequined Uggs, cramming them over the navy tights she wore with the only fashionable maternity dress she owned that still fit—she'd change into her navy pumps at the office. Early on in her pregnancy, she'd found cute, cheap dresses at thrift shops, but now that she was huge, secondhand maternity wear was as elusive as late-October real estate sales.

"Maybe you should stay in?" Gigi had moved on to a more current *Vanity Fair*.

Mr. Bojangles glared at the imposition of waking when she moved.

"Mom, stop." Tiffany added a pale pink cardigan over the dress, then a floral scarf and pearls. At this point, accessorizing was her only hope of maintaining a businesslike appearance at Hearth and Home Realty, where she worked twice as hard as her coworker Lyle, yet because he was the boss's nephew, he had a knack for landing the best listings. "We can't live in Maple Springs forever. Don't you want to get back to Dallas?"

"Honestly?" Gigi sighed. "I'd rather continue hiding. As long as Big Daddy's *away*, I'm not setting foot in polite society."

To this day—months after her husband's formal sentencing—Gigi refused to state out loud that her husband was in prison. She much preferred genteel euphemisms that sidestepped the harsh reality that it could be a year before she had a true marriage again.

Tiffany had visited her father only twice but regularly called.

Gigi preferred old-fashioned paper correspondence.

"I've got to get to a showing by nine. Try helping Grammy with some housework, okay?" Tiffany kissed her mother's cheek—already fully made up and smelling of pricey lotion and cream. To show how much she adored her mom, Tiffany picked up sample-sized expensive-brand cosmetics at Bismarck department stores or online at discount wholesalers. There was no need for Gigi to ever learn the true extent of just how bad things were financially.

"I'll try, dear, but you know how dust makes me sneeze."

"I know. Just do your best." Tiffany rubbed Mr. Bojangles between his ears, then made it down the two-story home's creaky front stairs and almost to the door before getting busted by her grandmother.

"Don't even think of dashing out of here without a proper breakfast."

"Grammy, I'm starving and would love to eat but have to meet a client by nine."

"What if I made you an egg-and-cheese sandwich to go?"

Tiffany's tummy growled. That did sound awfully tempting.

"See?" Grammy smiled. "Your boy's already got an appetite."

"Okay, I'll eat. But I'm meeting Mr. Jones at the office at nine, so I can't be late. And, Grammy, you know I can't keep the baby."

"Nonsense." Pearl guided Tiffany into the kitchen and parked her in a comfy chair at the table her ancestors had reportedly hauled west in a covered wagon.

She happily sighed when her grandmother handed her a steaming mug of homemade cocoa with whipped cream on top.

"Mmm… I love you," Tiffany said.

"I know," Pearl said.

When the first piece of bacon hit the skillet, Mr. Bojangles scurried into the kitchen. Of course, Grammy fed him part of a still-warm buttermilk biscuit.

The eggs frying in butter in her grand-mother's favorite cast-iron skillet smelled so good that Tiffany didn't even get too terribly upset when an extra-hard wind gust rattled the paned windows. She just glanced that way to note that it had indeed started to snow.

The flakes were huge—like designer gum-balls falling topsy-turvy, covering ugly brown grass with a tidy blanket of white.

Would her son love playing in the snow as much as she used to when visiting her grand-mother over the holidays?

Along with the realization that she'd never know, pain knotted the back of her throat. She squashed it.

Giving up her son was the hardest thing she'd

ever do, but it was hands down the best decision for *him*. For his future life. What she wanted didn't matter. If it did…

Well, she squashed that thought, too.

ROWDY LOVED STAYING with his folks, but having spent the bulk of the past ten years in warm—if not downright hot—climates, he much preferred the family traveling to Virginia to see him. A few times a year, they packed up his brother, Carl, sister-in-law, Justine, and their two rug rats, six-year-old Ingrid and eight-year-old Isobel, to come to the beach.

Clearly, the last time he'd been in Maple Springs had been a disaster. He'd always had a thing for cowgirls and Tiffany had been as hot as they come.

Last Easter had been unseasonably warm, and after the annual rodeo he'd attended, he and a few friends had headed to the town's only bar. He'd met Tiffany in one of those twists of fate you might see in movies but think never actually happen.

Rowdy had tried calling her, but the number had been disconnected. He'd next gotten on the phone with his mom and had her make a few discreet inquiries.

Rowdy had been under the impression that Tiffany lived in Dallas, but turned out a very pregnant girl named Tiffany Lawson currently resided with Pearl Lawson, who used to run the town's only grocery before selling it to the Dewitt brothers—all of which was a roundabout way of explaining why he was now headed down Buckhead Road to meet with Tiffany at her place of business at Hearth and Home Realty. If his mom ever gave up ranch life, she ought to consider signing on with the CIA. No spook Rowdy had met came close to solving a mystery like his mom.

That said, she was currently none too happy with him.

For quite a few years, she'd expected him to marry and give her more grandkids. The news that she might already have a grandson on the way had been far more agreeable to her than him. It hadn't been that long since he'd been through a similar scenario, and he couldn't handle that brand of stress again.

Regardless, he had plenty of leave time coming, so he'd let his CO know he'd be gone a few weeks, then hopped the earliest flight to Bismarck. His family had been thrilled to pick him up from there. That had been yesterday.

First on this morning's agenda was meeting with the mother of his child and hopefully having a rational, adult conversation about a number of topics. First, he needed to be 100 percent sure the baby was his. Second, he'd inform her that she had no right in hell to give his son away to strangers—or anyone else. That said, he wasn't sure what might happen next, but he was an honorable man.

He and Tiffany would find a mutually amenable arrangement.

His folks felt Rowdy should have at least given the woman a courtesy call that he was in town, but when it came to the topic of signing away his kid, he wasn't in a courteous mood.

In a businesslike setting, everyone would be on their best behavior.

The twenty-minute drive from the ranch to town gave him too much time to think.

Maple Springs was nice enough in the summer, but once winter set in, the place could best be described as gray. A half-mile, single-sided stretch of old-as-dirt grayish brick buildings housed antiques stores, insurance agents, the drugstore, the diner and café, three clothing stores, and a day care. A few years back, his mom told him the mayor's wife decreed the windows of each business be fitted with red-striped canvas awnings. In warmer months, they were okay, but the rest of the year, they resembled soggy ice- and snow-crusted circus popcorn boxes.

Judging by how fast the snow was falling, this might be one of the last weeks of the year when both sides of Richard L. Fulmer Avenue were available for parking. The usual snowplow drift grew on the same side of the road as the railroad tracks. That side also happened to not have any businesses—at least not until a good two miles outside town, where the Robert T. Fulmer Tavern had moved into the former feed store's building. Mayor Richard L. Fulmer was less than pleased about his twin brother serving spirits, which was why the establishment had to be outside city limits.

As long as the beer was cold, nobody in town gave two hoots. As an added bonus, Robert had been kind enough to restore the long-abandoned roadside motel just next door. Much to his brother's dismay, he'd been voted Maple Springs' Man of the Year in 1998 for giving free rooms to patrons too tanked to drive.

Rowdy recalled that at the time of his son's conception, he was awfully thankful for the motel's close proximity.

He pulled his dad's truck into an empty space just down from Hearth and Home's office. When he wasn't in town, Rowdy stored his truck in one of the ranch's outbuildings. As his lousy luck would have it, this morning, the damned thing hadn't started.

In an attempt to hold off winter's fast-approaching gloom, pumpkin lights hung from the office's awning. Skeletons danced from gaslight sconces on either side of the mirrored-glass double doors.

Rowdy turned off the engine, then sat a spell to compose his thoughts. He'd made his appointment with Tiffany through her secretary. Would Tiffany even remember who he was? For that matter, was she mistaking him for another man? There was also an off chance this gal wasn't even the same woman with whom he'd had relations. If she wasn't, he'd be free to return to his normally kick-ass life.

Forcing a deep breath, he dove from the balmy truck cab to the miserable white mess outside.

Sleet mixed with the snow.

Wind pitched it like darts against his forehead and cheeks. He tugged his battered brown leather cowboy hat lower and raised his long duster coat's collar higher.

Hell's bells, what he wouldn't give to be back in Virginia.

Everyone on the bustling street walked with their heads down. It was a downright miracle there weren't more pedestrian collisions.

He yanked open the door to find wondrous heat. It took a few seconds for his eyes to adjust to the sudden lack of sleet in them. When they did, he found a cozy seating area that had a sofa and two armchairs facing a coffee table and electric fireplace.

"Mr. Jones?" A woman with curly brown hair that was almost as big as her bosom rose from her desk to extend her hand. "Our Tiffany will be glad you made it through this storm. Sometimes newcomers take a while to adjust to our weather, don'tcha know."

"True. But I grew up here, so I'm used to it." Her thick accent had him working to hide a smile. When he'd lived in town, he hadn't noticed, but now that he'd been away, he heard how pronounced it was in some Maple Springs residents.

"You did? Well, why didn't you say so? Who are your people?"

"Patsy and James Jones. Know them?"

"As I live and breathe. *Rowdy?*"

"Yes, ma'am. Have we met?"

"Boy—you're breaking my heart." She pressed her hand to her impressive rack. "I'm

Doris Mills. Well, used to be Doris Patrick, but that was before I went and married Skeeter. I used to be your fourth-, fifth- and sixth-grade Sunday-school teacher. Don't you remember?"

"Sure. Sorry. It's been a while."

"I'll say." She looked him up and down, then whistled. "You've grown into a cool drink of water. Bet your momma's pleased as punch 'bout you moving home."

To avoid getting into the whole messy business of why he was actually in town, Rowdy said, "I, ah, really need to talk with Tiffany and figured having her show me a house or two would be the best way to connect."

"You two sweet on each other? You always did have the kindest heart. It's adorable that you don't mind her being…" she reddened and patted her own robust belly "…you know… By another man."

Ouch. "Would you mind pointing me to her office?"

"Oh—sure, sure." She waved toward a short hall. "Two doors down on your left."

"Perfect. Thanks."

Rowdy stood outside the partially closed office door for a good thirty seconds. He'd have felt more comfortable pulling all-night surveillance in croc-infested waters. This whole thing raised an uncomfortable number of similarities to a not-so-distant situation he'd just as soon forget. Besides, aside from what his brother had told him about the crap he'd gone through with Justine's cravings, mood swings and general crankiness, Rowdy knew nothing about pregnant women. That said, he did know a fair bit about charming the normal variety of gal and planned on using the same general logic.

"Thank you, Susie. Promise, as soon as I have my next sonogram, I'll email the pictures."

Eavesdropping on Tiffany's call, Rowdy narrowed his gaze.

"Susie, I'm expecting a client any second, but promise, I'll sign all of your attorney's documents this afternoon." There was a long pause. "Please stop worrying. I have no intention of backing out of the adoption. This baby boy will soon be yours."

"The hell he will." So much for adult professionalism or laying on the charm. Rowdy stormed Tiffany's office like an enemy camp—only instead of rescuing hostages or liberating territory, he was claiming his unborn son.

Chapter Two

"Susie, I've gotta go." After hanging up the phone, Tiffany's eyes widened in shock and maybe even a little horror to find her baby's daddy standing a mere five feet away. "You…"

The man she hadn't shared a room with since she could see her own toes closed the door.

"What are you doing here? How did you even find me?" Flustered, she couldn't decide what to do with her hands. She skimmed her no-doubt-messy hair, then tried crossing her arms, but that didn't feel quite right, because she'd grown so top-heavy that her arms were practically under her chin—yet one more reason to despise the man standing before her.

"Got your message." He wagged a silver-toned cell phone.

"Little late, aren't you?"

He shrugged. "Been out of town. Unavoidable delay."

"Uh-huh…" She returned to her email. "Whatever you've got to say, you're not just a *little* late, but *all-the-way* late. Adoption plans are already in place."

"About that…" He stepped forward, bracing his hands on either side of her small desk. In a quiet, downright lethal tone, he said, "There's no way in hell you're signing away my son."

Tiffany gulped. The last time she'd seen him he'd been handsome, but she'd also been wearing martini goggles and in hindsight had figured it was an impossibility for him to look half as good as she remembered. Wrong. He looked even better. He smelled amazing, too—like a day at the beach. Warm sun and sand and a hint of sexy sweat. She sneaked a peek at whisker-stubbled cheeks and eyes green enough to remind her of her former Dallas mansion's lawn.

Straightening in her chair, she retorted, "As a matter of fact, I am giving him up. We might have discussed the matter had you been courteous enough to call within hours—or even days—of my message. But when you failed to share so much as an opinion after months, what did you expect? As much as I'd love being a mom, I can barely afford being me—which reminds me, I have an appointment for a showing, so you'll need to leave."

He not only didn't leave but set his battered brown leather cowboy hat in one guest chair, then proceeded to help himself to the other. His legs were so long they didn't fold right given the cramped space, so he stretched them out.

Beneath her desk, the toes of his cowboy boots touched the toes of her pumps.

She lurched backward as if she'd been struck by a rattler.

"Let me guess?" he asked with a lopsided, white-toothed grin. "This client is a Mr. Jones?"

"Yes. You know him?"

"I am him." He chuckled.

"No, no, no..." She massaged her forehead.

"Oh, yes."

"But I needed that commission." Her stinging eyes and tight throat might mean she was ready to cry, but she refused to give him the satisfaction.

"Relax. I'll help you raise the baby. Financially, and you know . . ." He waved his hands. "With all the other stuff kids need."

"Great—only you won't be raising him at all. Susie and Jeb Parker will. They're amazing people, and both have real jobs—as opposed to you. I'm assuming you're a low-life seasonal cowboy? Now that you've earned enough cash to buy beer through the long, cold winter, you're back in town to raise a little hell?"

"First, cut the attitude and sass. Second, how about trying to act like a civilized adult. Third, I'm a freaking navy SEAL—it doesn't get much more *real* than that, sweetheart."

"You're in the navy? In the middle of North Dakota? The night we were together, you told me you were a bull rider. But now I see you meant to say you're just full of bull." She primly folded her hands atop her desk. What she wouldn't give to have one of her father's former legal team make mincemeat of this loser—although they hadn't been all that successful with her dad.

"Okay…" He sighed, then leaned back in his chair, opening his long duster coat just enough for her to see how well his brown sweater clung to his broad chest. "I get that the night we met,

I wasn't exactly on my best behavior, but then, neither were you."

True.

"But here's the deal. I really am in the navy, and I was in town for the annual rodeo and to visit my family for Easter. They were supposed to join me in Virginia Beach, but Dad tripped during the last big snow and hurt his back. The reason I never got your message is because I was in Afghanistan and dropped my damned phone down a well."

"Show me pics or it didn't happen." What kind of drugs was this guy on? "Oh—but since your phone is at the bottom of a well, guess that won't happen, either."

"Ever heard of the *cloud*?" His expression brightened when he pulled out his phone to start flipping through photos of a guy wearing desert camo, mirrored Ray-Bans and a similar cowboy hat, only with a full beard and shaggy hair. "Here I am with a donkey, and playing soccer with village kids—that's the phone-eating well in the background..." He pointed. "There's me driving a tank, and me in a cave— Oh, here I am with a cheetah. You find the damnedest things in terrorist camps."

"Okay, okay, so you proved you've been somewhere in the Middle East, but as for you being a SEAL? Let's get real. If I had a dollar for every time some guy in a bar told me he was a fighter pilot or spy—or in your case, bull rider—I sure wouldn't be selling real estate in the middle of nowhere, North Dakota."

"Case in point." He stashed his phone in his back pocket, then winked. "You sure didn't have a problem with my line the night we made our son—*if* he even is mine." He said the words, but Logan's churning stomach recalled that split second of condom doubt. He could deny it all he wanted, but in all probability, this baby was his.

She rolled her eyes.

"Ready to reach an amicable arrangement?"

"No. Because not only do I not believe you're from Maple Springs, but I think you're lying about the navy and your rodeo glory days and probably damn near everything else you've ever told me."

"That's it." Jaw clenched, he leaped to his feet, planted his hat on his head, then rounded to her side of the desk. Hand on her upper arm, he barked, "Get up. There's someone you need to meet."

"I'm not going anywhere with you."

"Oh, yes, you are."

"*No*, I'm not."

"Look…" Even though he'd released her, she could have sworn his each individual fingertip scorched her skin through her dress. He knelt so his gaze landed dead even with hers. He was close enough for his warm, coffee-laced breath to flare her nostrils and raise achingly familiar goose bumps up and down the length of her arms. To compensate for the fact that her lungs forgot how to breathe, she gasped—unfortunately making her sound like a flopping fish. Good God, he was a fine-looking man. "I understand why my showing up like this would catch you off guard, but promise, I have nothing but you and our baby's best interests at heart. If you want to share custody, I'll happily pay child support. If you want to go the old-fashioned route and get hitched, I'd hardly say I'm thrilled with the idea, but we could work something out. Come back to Virginia with me. I'm damned good-looking and you're a stone-cold fox. This baby's gonna be a heartbreaker. We'll make things legal. You stay home with the rug rat and I'll provide you both with a decent living. I get why you might not trust me, but since we already have an appointment, at least come with me to my parents' ranch. Meet my mom and dad—they'll vouch for me. Give me a chance to prove I'm a stand-up guy."

His speech made Tiffany more than a little miffed.

Their looks were irrelevant.

Besides, she had a plan. A good plan. He'd been out of her picture for months. How dare he barge in here and act like he was now in charge?

"What do you say? It's nasty outside, but Dad's got a fire going and Mom makes crazy-good hot chocolate. Toss in one of her home-made cinnamon rolls and I promise, you won't be disappointed."

What if I already am? Not by any of what he'd just proposed, but by the fact that it was far too late to put on the brakes and start over with their relationship. She never would have slept with the guy if something about him hadn't drawn her in. He was smart-mouthed and cocky and no doubt a pain in the ass to deal with in everyday life. But his green eyes made her feel as warm as if she were back home in Dallas, relaxed and happy, strolling hand in hand barefoot across a sumptuous grass lawn she hadn't had to mow.

"Tiff?"

"What happened to you thinking I'm lying about you being my baby's father? Plus, I don't even know your full name."

"Sorry. Now that I've seen you, I remember how we both went more than a little crazy that night. As for my name, it's Rowdy Jones. Right there on your appointment sheet." He nodded to the memo on her desk. Mr. Jones. He hadn't lied about his name?

"Show me your ID."

He shook his head at the imposition but did as she asked.

Sure enough, unless he'd spent a fortune on a fake, that was his real name. He stood six-two, weighed 220 and was even an organ donor.

"Now that you know I'm official, ready to meet my folks?"

She lurched when the baby gave an extra-hard shove to her appendix.

"Whoa…" Rowdy stared at her enormous belly. "Was that our little guy?"

She had a spiteful retort on the tip of her tongue about the baby technically no longer belonging to either of them, but Tiffany instead nodded.

"Mind if I…you know…" He hovered his hand above her bump.

"Knock yourself out."

When he touched her, all sense of logic short-circuited.

His fingers were big and warm and reminded her of that night when they'd both been very naughty, yet that poor behavior had felt so very good. She hadn't been with another man since.

The sad truth was that she hadn't wanted to.

This guy—the one she'd been reunited with

for all of fifteen minutes—was already making her head swim with all manner of delicious possibilities for a brighter, better life.

But she didn't have just herself to consider. Even if she did, she had to remember men were the enemy—*on all fronts*. Her dad had been a ticking time bomb for a decade before exploding her and her mother's lives. Then there was her ex, Crawford. Just when she'd needed him most, he'd emotionally shredded her heart. He hadn't even had the cojones to tell her in person that he wanted a divorce. He'd had some random court-appointed suit show up at their Dallas home to serve papers. She'd tried calling him, certain there had been a mistake, but his secretary had told her Crawford was no longer accepting her calls and that the house, the furnishings, her jewelry and a sizable chunk of cash were hers free and clear.

The only stipulation?

Crawford William Ridgemont IV wanted his precious, unsoiled family name back.

Devastated didn't begin to describe how she'd felt. She'd given him what he wanted, then proceeded to sell the house and everything in it to help pay Big Daddy's legal fees.

The baby kicked again—jolting her from the past and right back into her confusing present.

"Damn..." Rowdy whistled. "He's a tough little guy. We'll need to start thinking of names. My mom's already got a half dozen, but what would you think about John Wayne—of course, as a tribute to the legend."

"*John Wayne Jones?* Really?" Tiffany pushed her wheeled desk chair back so abruptly that Rowdy, who still had his hand pressed to her belly, lost his balance and fell onto his knees.

"Hell, woman." He rubbed his lower back. "What's your problem? A little advance notice of your move might've been nice."

"So would returning my call."

He groaned. "Are we back to that? I already told you about my phone and the well."

"Look," she said as she examined her sadly painted pink nails. "There's much more going on here than you could possibly understand. It's complicated." All her life, she'd had a private manicurist, and she still hadn't mastered the art of doing it herself. But she was trying— just like she was giving all she had to this real estate job. All she'd need was one good commission to build her savings and ensure Gigi and Pearl would be comfortable and warm for at least a few months if that was how long it took for her to make her next sale. "All my life, I've depended on men, and they've always, *always* let me down. Now the only person I trust with my well-being is *me*." She hugged her belly. "Don't think for one hot second I wouldn't love being a stay-at-home mom, but I've been down that road and discovered the hard way that it's a dead end."

"So you don't want to get married?" Was it her imagination, or did he look relieved?

"Excuse me?"

"I'm cool with you being a single mom. I mean, I'll always be there for you whenever I'm in the States and I plan to support my kid whether we marry or not, but it might be best if we don't tempt fate by— How do I put this in a delicate manner?" There he went again with his maddeningly sexy grin. "Let's just say it probably wouldn't be in either of our best interests to go at *it* quite to that degree again."

"Get out." She pointed toward her closed office door.

"Aw, now, don't go getting your pretty pink panties in a wad—I wasn't complaining. I just—"

She stood. "I don't care what you meant. And for the record, Mr. Jones, my panties are black—like a black widow spider. After she mates, she *kills*." Tiffany had once heard the line in a movie and thought it made for a great dramatic effect. She tried crossing her arms to further emphasize she meant business, but of course, they landed too high on the baby to be comfortable or sufficiently menacing. Still, no way was she giving in now. *"Get out."*

"Miss Tiffany, you are one helluva special snowflake." After a good long chuckle, he pushed himself to his feet, retrieved his hat, then followed her orders. "Want your door open or closed?"

"Closed."

"I'll be in touch."

Only after she was once again alone did Tiffany collapse back into her desk chair. During previous catastrophes, she might have indulged in a nice long cry, then soaked in a bubble bath with plenty of champagne and imported chocolates.

Now? Her only option was to pull out the big guns.

With an extra-hard tug, her bottom desk drawer popped open to reveal one of her favorite wedding gifts—a Baccarat crystal candy dish from Crawford's Aunt Cookie. Since they'd been married two years before their divorce, Tiffany got to keep all the gifts. She'd sold the vast majority but kept a cherished few. After all, now that she'd reached rock bottom, she needed to remember what awaited her back at the top.

Smiling, she reached into the bowl for one—okay, make that four—fun-sized Snickers.

Rowdy might have temporarily interrupted her day, but she refused to let him permanently bring her down. She had commissions to earn, a mother and grandmother to support, and a healthy baby to raise for the Parkers. Which was why she next ate a snack-sized bag of minicarrots, followed by apple juice and cheddar cheese cubes.

All of which should have filled her but didn't.

What was she really craving?

One of those cinnamon rolls Rowdy said his mom made.

Covering suddenly flushed cheeks, Tiffany rested her forehead against the cool laminate top of her desk. Given the fact that according to WebMD, the average cost of childbirth in America was $9,600—an uncomplicated C-section was a whopping $15,800—she had no option other than to give her son up for adoption so his new parents could pay. Pearl offered to mortgage her home to keep her great-grandson in the family, but Tiffany could no more let her do that than she could afford health insurance—she knew she'd owe a hefty penalty come tax time for not finding coverage, but she'd worry about that next April.

What Rowdy proposed sounded crazy. Maybe if he'd presented his proposition in a more reasonable manner, she might have considered it.

All she had to do to keep her baby was marry his father, and voilà—her every financial problem would vanish. Only it wouldn't be quite that easy. Rowdy wasn't going to make her his bride for nothing, and not to be a drama queen, but she'd already learned the price for marriage was her soul.

Chapter Three

"Uh-oh…"

"That about sums up my morning." Rowdy shut the back door on nasty blowing snow, wishing he were back on a beach—or, shoot, even a desert would be preferable to this.

"I take it she didn't accept your proposal? Told you so. You should've taken a ring." Patsy Jones lounged in the kitchen's usually sun-flooded window seat, wearing the Hello Kitty grown-up footy pj's his dad had bought her last Christmas. Maybe it was best he hadn't brought Tiffany today?

"Best as I could tell, her refusal had nothing to do with a ring." He hung his hat and coat on the rack beside the door, then went straight to the oven, only to find it empty. "Thought you were making cinnamon rolls?"

"I was, but in the book I'm reading, Jack just got chased by a bear and Marcy has his gun."

Shaking his head, Rowdy settled for heating up a can of SpaghettiOs, then asked, "Where are Dad and Carl?"

"They called a while ago. Found a momma determined to have her calf in this storm. They're staying out there to make sure she's okay."

"Cool." Only it wasn't. He was used to having every minute of his days filled with action, and out here, seemed like everyone had something to do but him. He'd planned on having the mother of his child here to at least hash out plans.

He was running out of time. He needed to get back on base, and their baby wasn't going to wait for Tiffany to make a decision. "I'll be in my room."

"Why? Don't tell me you're giving up?"

He sighed. "No way, but there's not a whole lot else I can do today. Since my ambush didn't work, I need to come up with a better plan of attack."

"How about if you don't treat this like one of your military missions but like a man asking a woman to marry him for the sake of their child? Did you tell Tiffany how sweet you can be if you set your mind to it?"

"I told her I was good-looking."

"Good grief, Rowdy. No wonder she's confused."

"More like pissed. From what I can gather,

this isn't her first rodeo, and she's been burned before."

His mom paled. "You mean she already has a child?"

"No. I meant her previous relationships went sour, so now she's one of those man-hater types."

Frowning, she noted, "I'm not sure what that means."

"You know—like the last guy she was with was an ass, so now she hates all men."

"That can't be true." She winced at his foul language, then rested her book on the nearest pillow. The kitchen was yellow, and by yellow, Rowdy meant every last thing save for the oak kitchen table and white marble counters was the color of a damned lemon. Her pillowed window seat was no exception. "Did you tell her you're not like that and wouldn't hurt her?"

"Sure, but by not contacting her until this late in the game, I pretty much already have hurt her. If only I'd have been here from day one of her pregnancy, you know?"

"That's a given. But it's not like you were off with another woman. Did you explain how your phone fell down a well?"

He snorted. "To Tiffany that was the equivalent of telling her my dog ate my homework. She's not buying it."

"Want me to talk to her? Vouch for you?" *Yes.* Initially, that had been exactly what he wanted. But now he wasn't sure bringing his mom into this mess would help.

"Thanks, but no." He arched his head back, slicing his fingers through his buzzed hair. "The last thing I want is for you to interfere."

She waved off his concern and ducked her head back behind her book.

In his room, Rowdy used the remote to click on the TV and flip through channels, but then he realized the TV no longer had a satellite connection—just an ancient VCR and a stack of his mom's workout and chick-flick tapes.

His desk had been replaced by a treadmill, and against the wall where his bed used to be now sat a sewing/craft station and a brass daybed with a freakin' yellow floral spread. His formerly blue walls had been painted yellow and his bikini pinups no doubt burned.

Outside, the storm raged on.

He felt restless and in a perfect world would have saddled his paint, Lucky, to go help his dad and brother. But the odds of finding them in this whiteout were slim to none, which landed him stuck in his yellow cage.

Needing a male perspective, he called Logan. The team was off for another week. Knowing his friend, he was either sleeping, playing PS4 or deep into strip beach bingo with some hottie he'd picked up at Tipsea's, the local SEAL hangout.

"Dude." Logan answered after the third ring.

"I was just on a Yuengling and chip run for a 'Call of Duty' marathon—saw a pregnant chick at Food Lion and thought of you. How's it going?"

"Tiff's last words to me were *Get out.*" What Rowdy wouldn't give for just one of their fave local beers.

"Damn. You've always got game. If you're not getting action with your own baby momma, there's no hope for the rest of us schmucks."

"Ha ha." Rowdy walked to the room's picture window and pressed his forehead to the cool glass. "What should I do?"

"All women are suckers for presents. I say buy her a bunch of flowers and pickles and ice cream—whatever pregnant chicks like."

"Have you seen the flower assortment up here? This is North Dakota we're talking about. There might be a couple wilted red truck-stop roses, but that's about it."

"You're making excuses, man. I'm telling

you, buy her something nice. Works every time."

Rowdy grimaced.

He'd have gotten better advice from his horse.

Should he have called Duck? Nah. Rowdy didn't need another lecture on the virtues of being a family man. He was a soldier. It was the only thing he knew how to do.

After a few minutes' more small talk with Logan, he hung up to pace.

In a roundabout way, maybe Logan's idea wasn't so bad. Rowdy just needed to take that gifting to the next level.

How many times had Tiffany mentioned that she'd intended to show him houses? He could stay in the navy for only so long and, after retirement, had always planned on returning home. He had money stashed away. What if he went ahead and bought a retirement cabin now? Not only would Tiffany get the commission, but he'd have all that house-hunting time with her to foster goodwill.

Heck, she and his son could even stay in the place when he was deployed. His mom would be close enough to check on her—as would her own mother and grandmother.

From where he was standing, the idea looked like a win-win.

So much so that he headed back downstairs for his hat, coat, boots and keys.

After a little legwork netted him Tiffany's grandmother's address, he announced his new plan to his mom. She gave him grief about driving in the storm, but he was a SEAL.

No way would he be stopped by a little snow…

"OHMYGOSH!" GIGI STEPPED back from the front door to allow space for a snow-covered man to stumble inside Pearl's foyer. "You must be freezing. Get in here. I'm not accustomed

to welcoming strange men into my home, but in this case, it's the only charitable thing to do." Once he was inside, she shut the door on a growling north wind and blowing snow. *"Tiffany! Mother!"*

"I'm right here," Tiffany said from behind her mom. "There's no need to shout." Especially since this man was no stranger, but Rowdy.

"You stupid man." Tiffany took his hat and coat, hanging them on the brass rack at the base of the stairs. Both of his personal items were snow crusted. "Why are you out in this storm? More importantly, what are you doing here?"

Mr. Bojangles yapped at Rowdy's boots.

"I—I got a g-great idea." His teeth chattered so bad he could hardly speak. Ice crystals clung to his stubble and his cheeks had turned an alarming red.

"You know him?" Gigi asked.

"Yes." Tiffany would have loved telling a

little white lie, but apparently Rowdy's deter-mination outweighed her imagination.

"You never told me you had a suitor." Gigi beamed as if she'd been handed the keys to the Dallas Galleria Neiman Marcus. "How very nice to meet you. I'm Mrs. Gregoria Hastings-Lawson, but my friends call me Gigi."

"Mom, could you please find some towels."

"Oh, of course." She scampered off.

The dog licked from the rapidly forming snow puddle on the entry hall floor.

With her buttinsky mother temporarily out of the way, Tiffany snapped, "For heaven's sake, Rowdy, sit down and take off your wet boots—then let's get you in front of the fire."

He shivered too hard to be of much use, so she pushed him onto a small wood bench, then struggled to remove his icy cowboy boots for him.

"You do know you're crazy?" she scolded. "I had a tough time getting home after we talked, and that was pushing three hours ago. We're supposed to get twenty inches by morning."

"Swell…" His grin raised all manner of havoc in her tummy. For a woman who'd sworn off men, this was not a welcome development. "If we're snowed in together, we'll have plenty of time to come up with a game plan for keeping our baby."

"You're my future grandson's father?" Poor Gigi was past due for her Botox. How did Tiffany know? Because her mother's eyebrows rose an inch! "Why didn't you say so? But after you answer that, how about telling me where you've been. And then get this fool idea out of my daughter's head about giving my grandson up for adoption. A child doesn't need money to be loved. Tiffany's daddy grew up right here in Maple Springs and look how well he turned out—well, aside from his temporary setback. But—"

"Mom, please stay out of this."

"I will not."

"What's all the commotion?" Pearl wandered into the fray. She wore a quilted pink house-coat, slippers and a pink shower cap over her rollers, and her face was white with face cream. "*Ooooh*, how nice. Last thing I expected was to find a hottie in the house."

Tiffany closed her eyes, praying when she opened them, she'd find herself awaking from a bad dream. No such luck.

As if knowing he'd just made significant forward momentum in his mission, Rowdy delivered his stupid-handsome grin to all of the ladies, then held out his hand to her grandmother. "You must be Miss Pearl? My momma said she's never tasted a finer pumpkin pie than the one you made for the garden club's fall bake sale."

"Aren't you the charmer?" Pearl held his hand way longer than Tiffany deemed necessary. "If you don't mind my asking, who is your mother?"

"Patsy Jones. I'm her youngest, Rowdy. You've probably met my big brother, Carl? He helps my dad with our ranch and is married to a real sweetheart—Justine. She's a part-time teller down at First Trust Bank."

"Goodness gracious, what a small world. I've had my savings and checking accounts there for going on forty years. Now, since I'm older than dirt but not dumb as a box of rocks, what is this I heard about you being the father of my great-grandson. Is this true?"

"Yes, ma'am." He had the audacity to meet Tiffany's stare. "But I swear on my own grandmother's grave, I only recently heard of your beautiful granddaughter even being pregnant. I'm in the navy and have been overseas. But as soon as I got the news, I caught a flight, and here I am. Just this morning, I proposed to your granddaughter—told her if she wanted,

I'd make an honest woman of her, but she flat turned me down."

Oh—he played dirty.

Pearl and Gigi both stood mooning with their hands pressed to their chests.

"I can't tell you what a relief that will be." Gigi freed one hand from her bosom to fan her flushed cheeks. "I don't consider myself old-fashioned, but nothing would make me happier than to see Tiffany married before the baby comes. Of course, she's already been married once before, but we don't speak of that."

"Mom!" Tiffany gave her a glare before turning back to their uninvited, unwelcome guest. "Rowdy, I'm not sure why you're here, but pretty sure it's time for you to go."

"Nonsense." Pearl turned for the stairs. "Give me a sec to gussy up, and then I'll make everyone a nice late lunch. Or would that be an early supper? Either way, we'll have plenty to discuss, what with a wedding and baby shower to plan."

"There's not going to be either, Grandma. We've already been over this a dozen times."

"Sounds good, Miss Pearl. My ride got stuck a ways back, and I worked up a powerful hunger walking through the snow."

"Oh, dear," Gigi said. "Sounds like you'll have to stay on for dinner and maybe even breakfast, too."

"But I do expect him to take the downstairs guestroom," Pearl noted. "Just because the rooster got into the henhouse once, doesn't mean it needs to happen again until I see a ring on our Tiffany's finger."

"Yes, ma'am." Rowdy nodded. "I couldn't agree more." As if just now noticing Mr. Bojangles, he knelt to scoop up the tiny dog. Had her traitorous mutt been a cat, he'd have purred from the scratching beneath his fussy collar.

"Aren't you a silly little thing? You're smaller than our baby's going to be."

"Correction—the Parkers' baby." Before her mind's eye filled with visions of handsome Rowdy cradling their son in his big, strapping arms, Tiffany snatched her dog, who growled during the transaction. "I already told you, we can't keep this baby."

"I told you we're going to reach a mutually amenable arrangement."

"Well, that's settled." Gigi handed Tiffany the towels. "Darling, how about you help your fiancé dry off and get comfy in front of the fire—then I'll get his room ready. Maybe after that, we can all play canasta? Rowdy, sugar, what do you think?"

"Sounds like a fine plan," Pearl said. "Only thing I love more than cards is a wedding."

The second her mother and grandmother left the entry, Tiffany landed a swift kick to Rowdy's left shin.

"Ouch," he complained. "What was that for?"

From his safe perch in the crook of her arm, Mr. Bojangles barked at the commotion.

"What do you think? Those two women mean the world to me, and because of your big fat mouth—" she kicked his right shin, too "—now they both have expectations that there's no way on God's green earth we'll ever be able to fulfill."

"Hate to burst your bubble, but at the moment, God's earth is white as driven snow."

She pitched the towels at him. "Dry yourself. I need to sit down."

"Is everything okay? With the baby, I mean?"

"Our son is fine. As for my rising blood pressure? That's a whole nother story."

"Knock, knock." Quarter past ten that night, after an endless day of trying to make Tiffany remember why she'd been hot enough for him to have even made a baby, Rowdy cracked open her bedroom door and poked his head through. "You decent?"

"No!" Her whispered word was more like a hiss.

Mr. Bojangles woke to go into yapping attack mode at the foot of her bed.

Rowdy entered and shut the door behind him.

"Go away!" She sat up in a big white wrought iron bed, pulling a comfy-looking stack of quilts up to her neck. "I want Mom and Grammy Pearl to at least pretend I'm a virgin."

He cracked a smile, then grabbed the dog. "Pretty sure that cat's *way* out of the bag. The night we met—that trick you did with my… *Damn.* Woman, you've got skills."

"Stop." She covered her blazing cheeks with her hands. "Why are you here? And I'm not just talking about being in my bedroom."

"Why do you think?" Cradling the dog just as sweetly as a baby, he perched on the empty side of the double bed. "I'm here to change your mind about that adoption. Hell, if you don't want your own son, I'll raise him myself. This morning, I gave you plenty of acceptable scenarios, and now you need to choose."

When tears welled in her eyes, she looked away. The sight of him with the dog was all too easy to get tangled up with other images in her mind. Her yappy, spoiled mutt wasn't the same as a real baby. Mr. Bojangles didn't need health insurance or diapers. For her family, times were so hard that Pearl had to barter eggs for a neighbor's bacon. There was no way Tiffany could ever afford to keep her child.

"Look." He softened his tone. "I get that when I didn't call you back, you assumed I was some derelict deadbeat, and I'm sorry. But I'm here now, and if you want me to break the news to that couple you made the adoption arrangement with, I'll do it. For the sake of the baby, if you want to get hitched tomorrow, I'm on board. Whatever decision you make is fine as long as I'm part of the equation."

"You don't understand." She took a roll of toilet paper from her bedside table, then tore off a piece to blow her nose. "The night you and I hooked up, I was out of my mind with grief and trying to mask the pain. My dad had been sent to prison and my husband divorced me right down to the point that he bought back his name. I went from a life of pampered luxury to blowing my nose with toilet paper." Borderline hysterical while still trying to whisper, she waved the roll around. "It's not even a good brand, but generic. Every dime to my name went to paying off Daddy's lawyers and now I've gone from my biggest worry being what color to paint my nails or how many calories were in my morning latte to being responsible for an entire household. I *hate* my ex. And I'm not especially fond of my dad, so forgive me if I don't buy your whole marriage scenario. We slept together—one night. So how in the world do you think I'm now ready to marry you?"

"Technically, we were together about six times that one night. And I'm not suggesting this is anything other than a solution to keep our baby. Marriage would be a means to a mutually beneficial end. That's all."

She pitched a lacy pillow at him, which he easily dodged.

Now her own dog growled at her!

"Sorry. Sounds like you've been through a rough patch, but—"

"*Rough* patch?" She was back to whisper-screeching. "I went through hell. I became that woman in Junior League and in my sorority's alumni chapter who everyone whispers about being one martini shy of having a nervous breakdown. The men I trusted the most yanked my world out from under me, so forgive me if I'm not feeling warm and fuzzy about a total stranger's vow to make me a live-in nanny. I don't know you from Adam. You could be an ax murderer or…or…shoplifter."

"Yeah." He nodded with a faint smile. "If I turned out to be one of those creepy guys who stash candy bars and gum in their pants that would be seriously bad news."

"You know what I mean."

"I do." He inched close enough to cup his hand over their baby. Even through layers of quilts, she felt a connection to him—to their son. Her every muscle tensed to resist the havoc his simple touch had created. "But here's the deal. I'm actually a really great guy, and if you'd give me a chance, I'd—"

"Tiff?" Gigi knocked, then opened the door. "Rowdy. I didn't expect to find you in my daughter's boudoir."

"Sorry, ma'am. Your daughter and I needed to talk—in private."

"About the wedding? Let's have a holiday theme. It'll be extra special, don't you think?"

"Sure," he said as if more determined than ever to see this crazy thing through.

"In that case…" She treated them to a huge wink. "I'll leave you two lovebirds alone. I need to start planning."

"Thank you." Rowdy smiled.

She smiled back and was gone.

Tiffany, however, was not smiling. If anything, her mood had turned even darker than it had been before.

"Now that I have your mother's blessing," he said, "will you at least meet my family before condemning me to the land of evil shoplifters?"

"Joke all you want." For an instant, she laughed. "But I'm serious. At any time you choose, you can walk away. I don't have that luxury. I also don't have the money to pay for our baby's birth, let alone diapers and college."

"Are you planning to have the baby at Regional Hospital here in town?"

"Yes." It was small but had a great reputation.

"If we're married, my health insurance will cover you."

"What then? I don't mean to sound bitchy, but what about everything else our baby boy is going to need—including time to care for him and love him and teach him to be a man? Let's say you are in the navy, and we marry. What happens if I hate Virginia? Or you?"

"A distinct possibility," he teased, patting her belly.

"This seems like a game to you—a challenge to win your son—but if you'd for one second be serious and think about the ramifications involved, I think you'd agree adoption is best for us both."

"Never. I was raised to accept my responsibilities. I was man enough to help create this baby, and I'll be man enough to raise him."

"But *why*? You've admitted how much your career means. Having a wife and child will only get in your way. Don't you get it? This adoption gives you an honorable out. Our baby will no longer be merely a responsibility but a blessing. The Parkers are wonderful, deserving people who will be better parents than you and I ever could."

"Look, you admitted you've had a rough year. Well, you're not the only one. What I'm about to share with you, even my parents and brother don't know…"

Chapter Four

Tiffany leaned closer. Did it make her an even more horrible person that one of the simple things she most missed about her former life was gossip? "Well? What could be so horrible?"

"Lord... Where do I even start?" He swallowed hard, rubbing her sleeping, traitorous dog behind his ears. When tears shone in Rowdy's green eyes, guilt had her offering the toilet paper roll. Whatever he was about to share, it was serious.

"Most people say start at the beginning, but I have a short attention span, so jump right in with the juicy parts."

He grinned.

She nearly swooned. *Baby, your daddy's a looker...*

"Anyone ever told you you're a little kooky?"

"All the time." She settled a pillow behind her back. "Now spill."

"Okay, but don't think badly of me. Because seriously, no one hates me more than me."

That didn't sound good, but who was she to cast stones? "Considering I got knocked up from a one-night stand, this is a judgment-free zone."

After a deep inhale, then slow exhale, words tumbled too fast, as if he'd been holding them in for far too long. "The night we met? Part of the reason I was so damned drunk was another woman. Back in Virginia, Brandi and I dated on and off—nothing serious. Then she tells me she's pregnant and the baby's mine."

Now Tiffany sucked in a deep breath. "Where's the infant and his or her momma now?"

"That's just it…" He rubbed the back of his neck. "We hardly had a great love story. It was all about sharing a few Friday-night drinks, then releasing the week's tensions. But hell, when she told me she was carrying my baby, I was prepared to do right by her and my kid. I bought her a ring, got down on one knee—the whole nine yards."

She leaned in closer. "Why aren't you married to her now?"

"Damn, woman, if you'd quit interrupting, I'd tell you."

"Sorry." To stop herself from blurting about a dozen more pertinent questions, Tiffany drew her lower lip into her mouth and bit.

"So anyway, I wasn't exactly proud of how

this whole thing was going down, but we got married, and then I got shipped out. Making a long story real short, by the time I got back, she'd had the baby—a boy. I had a son. I'd had a couple hundred sleepless nights to ponder what it was going to be like when I got home— you know, taking on the role of dad and husband to this infant and woman I hardly knew."

Where in the world was this going?

"Back on base, when I stepped off our C-130 transport, she waited for me on the tarmac with all of the other wives. When I caught my first sight of her with a baby stroller—not gonna lie—I could've downed an entire bottle of Pepto. Still, she was my wife, this was my son, and I was determined to be a great dad and partner. All around us, my SEAL buddies were making out with their wives or hugging their kids, so I got into it. Or at least tried. I kissed her cheek, then reached into the stroller for my son. Only when I picked him up for our first hug, I got a helluva shock—there was no way this kid could be mine."

"*What?* How could you tell?" Tiffany could deny it all she wanted, but when it came to juicy gossip, she was every bit as bad as her mother. This story was getting *good*.

"Let's just say the little guy was cute as a button but looked more like Bruce Lee than me. As far as I knew, we didn't have any Asians on the family tree. She admitted to having slept with another guy around the same time as me and that she was already back together with him. She pulled a packet of divorce papers from a pouch on the back of the stroller. Told me that once I signed them, our marriage would be officially over, then wished me a nice life. After all those nights I'd spent worrying about how I was going to perform as a father, just like that, the issue was off the table."

"Whoa…" Out of habit, Tiffany rubbed her baby bump. "You weren't kidding. That was nuts. But how does what Brandi did make you feel bad about yourself?"

"Because I was an idiot for landing myself in that situation. I'd always worn protection with her, but accidents happen. Now here I am again, facing the same issue with you. But the funny thing is, after another long-ass tour filled with way too much time for thinking, now maybe I am ready to be a dad."

"Do you know how crazy that sounds? After what that woman put you through, I would have figured you felt like she'd given you a get-out-of-jail-free card. I'm now offering you another one."

"But I want my son."

Tiffany shook her head. "You only think you want to be a dad. Trust me, I have bouts of suffering from baby fever, too. When those adorable diaper and baby-food ads pop up on TV, the chubby-cheeked close-ups get me teary eyed every time. But those aren't the realities of raising a child. To do right by him, to put the same time, attention and love into your son as you do being a SEAL, you might have to give up your career and move back to this dead-end town."

"Funny you mentioned that…" He set the dog between them, then cupped his hand over her belly. His palm created a warmth like a heating pad. When his barest touch felt this good, what if he spooned her? Warmed her entire aching back?

No, no, no. She might be able to squelch this impractical line of thought, but she didn't remove his hand. Selfishly, the much-needed comfort felt too good.

"I've always liked this town. I've seen a lot of the world—and granted, Paris and the Mediterranean have their perks. But honestly, there's an awful lot of ugliness out there, too. Here I'd have nothing but blue sky and the faces of everyone I love."

"And snow. You forgot about the multiple *feet* of snow."

He laughed.

"And what if this baby turns out to be not yours? Remember your not-so-nice implication that I'd made a mistake? You said as much back at my office."

"Sorry. The last thing I meant to imply was that you'd been sleeping around. I was there the night this little guy was conceived." He now added an infuriatingly distracting rub to her tummy. "I clearly remember being so hot for you that I was too out of my freakin' mind to make sure the condom was—well... How do I put this? Positioned correctly?"

Hot didn't begin to describe their chemistry. *Volcanic.*

Seismic.

Cataclysmic. All sorts of *-ic* words. And now that there was a baby on the way, *apocalyptic* also applied. Before she found out she was pregnant, life had still been a disaster but at least manageable. Now? Her sheer size made most tasks three times tougher than usual. As for the pang in her heart each time the baby kicked? That was the worst. Of course she wanted to keep their baby—more than anything. But logic dictated that wasn't going to happen.

"Since you're already knocked up, why not at least try seeing if we still share a connection?" He leaned closer, all the while stroking her tummy with his thumb.

Had there ever been a more idiotic question? They didn't share just a *connection* but the kind of explosive spark she'd never even experienced with her former husband—which was probably why they were now divorced. Rowdy's warm breath tickled her upper lip, goading her into all manner of naughty thoughts.

"We could pick up right where we left off…"

He shifted the dog lower on the bed, then

inched still closer until the empty space between them couldn't have been thicker than the flyer she'd found on her car window the night after having made the poor choice of being with him.

Why wasn't her dog defending her?

And speaking of poor choices…

The memory of seeing her positive pregnancy test served as a much-needed bucket of cold water to her flaming cheeks. Tiffany backed away. "You should probably go downstairs. If Grammy catches you up here, there's gonna be hell to pay."

He leaned forward, nuzzling her neck. "I never did mind dancing with the devil. Besides, I could tell straightaway your grandmother and momma like me just fine."

"I wouldn't take it too personally." Tiffany crossed her arms. "They'd love the trashman if he'd make an honest woman of me. They're both old-school and believe a woman has no business being pregnant without a wedding ring."

"So? Let's get one. First thing in the morning. Then, come afternoon, you can get to work finding us a house."

"Stop. Are you even listening to yourself? Rowdy, you're free. The Parkers are taking our baby and giving him a better life than we ever possibly could. He'll have the best of everything. Private school. Travel. Art lessons and dressage and speaking five foreign languages. Don't you want that for him? Don't you want him to have more than two parents who—up until this morning—didn't even know each other's last names?"

"While all of that fancy stuff sounds dandy, it doesn't hold a candle to true family ties. I'll be a great dad. I've already been practicing for damn near a year."

"Yay for you. But I can't be a mom—not yet. Maybe not ever. I already have one failed marriage, a father in prison, a mother teetering on the edge of a nervous breakdown and a grandmother who refuses to see the bad in anyone, when I can't remember the last time I had a man tell me the truth—present company excluded. I think. *Hope.*" She shook her head. "It doesn't matter. No matter what you say about anything, I'm not changing my mind about the adoption."

"Sorry, angel, but that decision's not entirely up to you. I have rights, too, you know?" He cupped his hand possessively over the baby. "This decision isn't just about you. We went over this at your office."

She sighed. "Please, just go."

He stared at her for the longest time.

The dim lamplight showed a weariness in him that she hadn't before seen. Shadows beneath his eyes and a sad downward turn to his lips. He was heartbreakingly handsome. Long lashes and those grassy-green eyes that called to mind sunny days spent downing Long Island ice teas on the sidelines of polo fields. What would a man like Rowdy have been like in her former world? Would she have given him the time of day?

She was so caught up in his stare that she forgot to breathe. When her body forced her to remember, her gulp went down too fast and left her coughing.

He was instantly by her side. "You okay?"

Still unable to speak, she nodded.

"We'll continue this discussion in the morning. Only you need to be ready to make concessions." Without waiting for her reply, he turned for the door.

No. He couldn't just waltz in here and dictate what she could and couldn't do. But she was tired of talking in circles, so she kept her mouth closed. Unfortunately, there was a lone question hammering at her like a woodpecker against a rickety wood shed. "Rowdy?"

"Yeah?" He didn't bother facing her.

"What did your parents say about your first marriage?"

"Not a damned thing. They don't know." With that shocker, he exited her room and shut the door.

More confused than ever, she scooped up the dog to settle him on his pillow beside her, then covered him with his own leopard-print fuzzy blanket. She turned out her bedside lamp, bunched a pillow between her legs and one behind her back and three more behind her head but still couldn't get comfortable— not the way she'd been with Rowdy alongside her for support.

Why hadn't he told his folks about his first baby scare? Embarrassment? Pride? But that morning, he'd offered right away to drive her over to meet his mom. Why? What about their situation made such a huge difference?

The old her—the Tiffany who'd believed

in happy endings—might have wondered if Rowdy had been looking for more from their union than she had, which was basically one night free from the nightmare that had become her life.

Running her hands over her belly, she closed her eyes and tried sleeping, but peace refused to come. Her lower back ached, and she was hungry and had to pee.

After a trek to the restroom, she carefully made her way down the back stairs to the kitchen. A mug of hot cocoa and a half-dozen of her grandmother's oatmeal cookies would be delicious. After that, she'd pop the rice bag she used as a heating pad into the microwave and then try going back to bed.

At the base of the stairs, she traipsed down the hall and into the kitchen, only to come to an abrupt stop.

Rowdy's entirely too-fine muscular legs and derriere clad in red-striped boxers were the only parts of him visible behind the open fridge door.

She'd just turned to tiptoe her way back up the stairs when the fridge door slammed.

"Jeez, woman!"

She spun around as fast as a seriously preggers woman could to find Rowdy clutching his chest.

"You scared the hell out of me."

"Sorry. I assumed you'd be sleeping."

"I should be, but you've got me so wound up on about eighty different topics that I'm having to stress-eat."

"You're wound up? How do you think I feel? I'm starving." She nudged him aside to make her way to the fridge.

"For the sake of both of our growling stomachs, let's table all topics involving the baby and focus on food. Deal?"

He held out his hand for her to shake.

She should have known better than to touch him again.

The instant she pressed her palm to his, a warm tingle didn't just take hold but threw her slightly off balance, as if she were standing on the bow of a yacht when it crashed down from a wave. He was without a doubt bad for her—in the most maddeningly wonderful way. All the more reason to steer clear of him.

After breaking their brief hold, she asked, "Want me to make you a sandwich?"

"Sit." He clamped his hands over her shoulders, aiming her toward the round oak table and nearest ladder-back chair. "Your grandmother's dinner was so good that I don't see the point in messing with perfection, do you? Leftovers sound awesome."

Trying not to get caught staring at his ridiculously toned body, she nodded.

Outside, wind howled.

Gusts made the old house shiver.

But inside, Pearl kept the propane heat on a tropical high. Refilling the tank wasn't cheap, which reminded Tiffany just how much she needed to make a house-sale commission.

"Tell me about your husband." He cradled four Tupperware bowls in his arms, then dropped them all onto the gold-speckled laminate counter. His biceps were big, but not bodybuilder beefy.

Her cheeks flamed from the memory of wrapping her fingers around them while he'd—

"Sorry. I see you're turning red. Was that too intimate of a question for our first late-night snack?"

She inwardly groaned. *Would it be too much to ask for you to put on some clothes?*

"Okay… Since that subject's apparently off-limits, I'll—"

"No," she said, fanning her flushed face with a coupon circular Pearl must have left on the table. "It's not like that. I'm having a hot flash." *Caused by you!* "Crawford and I were the ultimate cliché. We met at the University of Texas. His fraternity was always paired with my sorority. Our parents ran in the same social circles. We both had the same ambitions. He wanted to conquer the business world. I wanted to rule the Junior League and raise gorgeous babies. Looking back on it, I guess the whole thing was a big, shallow mistake. He's already remarried and aside from the embarrassment of the whole thing, I'm not all that heartbroken."

"You mentioned earlier that he broke things off because of your father's conviction?"

"Yep. I should have at least cheated or something, you know? At least given him a true reason for the split."

"If you don't mind another question, what's your dad locked up for?"

"Insider trading."

He nodded. "Ever planning on going back

to Texas?" Now that the lids were off all of the containers, he opened three cabinets before finding the one holding her grandmother's white china plates.

"Honestly?" A strangled laugh escaped her. "Sometimes when I can't sleep, I have visions of gliding back into town behind the wheel of a brand-new Jaguar convertible. My hair and nails and outfit will be flawless and I won't rely on a man for my well-being, since I'll run my own real estate empire."

"Nice." He spooned heaping portions of mashed potatoes, meat loaf and peas onto both plates.

"For the record—what this Crawford character did was pretty shitty. Sounds like a total douche bag. I mean, hell, he married you—not your dad."

"No kidding, right?" Her respect for Rowdy rose by a considerable margin. He could just be blowing happy smoke up her skirt, but his words seemed as genuine as his sympathetic smile. A problem, since the last thing she wanted was to be reminded of why she'd spent the night with him in the first place.

He popped one plate into the microwave, then joined her at the table with bowls of ambrosia and three-bean salad. He handed her a spoon. "Dig in."

"Thanks." She did. Never had she been more grateful for her grandmother's overabundance of side dishes at any given meal. "Mmm..." she said after swallowing her first bite of the sweet fruit salad. "When I was a kid, we used to always have this for special occasions."

"Should I take it as a compliment that Pearl made it for me on an ordinary Monday night?" His slow and easy grin was potent enough to steal her next breath.

They ate in companionable silence until both small bowls were empty. She was caught off guard by how much she enjoyed the simple pleasure of sharing a meal with him. Why was it that the harder she fought to resist him, the more he drew her in without the least bit of effort?

The microwave beeped.

She offered to get the one plate and put the other in, but he insisted on serving her, right down to delivering a napkin and fork.

"Thank you." She waited until they both had their meals to start in on hers.

"Don't wait on my account," he said. "Need anything else? Salt or pepper? Ketchup?"

"No, thank you. This is perfect."

The baby gave her an extra-hard kick. Surprise had her grasping her belly.

"Everything okay?" He eyed where she held her hands. "You're not having contractions, are you?"

"No. He just practiced his favorite soccer move. Nothing I can't handle."

Not bothering to ask permission, Rowdy

knelt alongside her chair, framing their son with his big hands, then leaning forward to rest his cheek to her womb.

Their son.

Her heart twisted from the rush of affection she felt for the man and unborn child—neither of whom would ever belong to her.

Chapter Five

"You're up awfully early."

"Yes, ma'am." Rowdy had hoped to sneak out before the three women of the house were awake, but Tiffany's grandmother was an early riser. "I figured since the storm passed, I should get a head start on digging out my truck."

Sun shone on the sea of white visible beyond red gingham curtains. The sky was a deep, clear blue. According to his phone, the temperature would be in the forties by noon, so thankfully, the snow would melt as fast as it had fallen.

"Wise idea. But you're not going anywhere without a nice rib-sticking breakfast."

"Thanks." He didn't dare tell her he was still full from all the food he and Tiffany had put away the previous night. Man, oh man, could that girl eat. If her appetite was any indication, their son would be a bruiser. "Anything I can help with?"

"Since you asked, I'd be much obliged if you'd gather the eggs and make sure the chickens have feed and their water didn't freeze. The coop is just around back. You might also check their heat lamp once you're out there."

"Will do." He was glad for the busywork. It might at least give him a fighting chance of forgetting the feel of his son moving just beneath his hands.

If things were different between him and Tiffany, she might have welcomed him, placing her hands atop his to press him closer, instead of stiffening at his every touch. As it was, he'd guessed he was crossing a personal-space boundary but didn't much care. He'd already missed the first seven months of his son's life and he'd be damned if he'd miss one day more.

In the front hall, he slipped his feet into his boots, then shrugged on his coat and added his cowboy hat and gloves.

He trudged through two feet of wet snow before reaching the chickens. Their coop was a fussy yellow shed that he figured his mother would very much like, given her affinity for the color. A flower box hung askew beneath a paned window and the wooden shingled roof had turned green with moss.

Near the latch-hooked door, he spotted a lidded feed bin and opened it to get a scoop. The grains smelled good. Familiar and sweet. While for the most part, there wasn't much about his life as a SEAL that he didn't enjoy, he had to admit to missing quite a bit about growing up on his family's ranch.

He ducked his six-foot-two-inch frame through the coop's low door to find the Araucana ladies not happy about his intrusion. Cozy in their straw-filled roosting shelves, they squawked and squabbled. A rooster strutted close enough to land a peck to Rowdy's shin.

"Hey," he protested, closing the door on the chill. Judging by the muggy heat and glow, the heat lamp was working just fine. "Don't peck the legs that are attached to the hands feeding you."

He shook grain into a shallow food tray, checked that the water hadn't frozen, then gathered ten blue eggs, which he held in his sweater's upturned hem. How amazing would it be to perform these chores with his son? To teach him about different breeds. He might enjoy Easter Eggers—they laid huge eggs that ranged from rose and blue to green and brown.

Rowdy's boy could raise his own chicks for a 4-H project.

Rowdy wanted his son with a visceral pull on his heart.

After what he'd been through with his first stab at parenthood, he now actually felt ready. Excited. How could he get Tiffany to feel the same?

The rooster delivered another peck to his shin.

"Thanks, buddy. You're making me feel about as welcome as Tiffany."

Rowdy left the coop to deliver the eggs to Pearl.

"You are a sweetheart," she said with a big smile. "I can't tell you what a treat it is to have a big, strapping man around the house. I have my suitors, but they mostly come by for pie and sugar." She winked. "If you know what I mean."

It took him a sec, but Rowdy eventually

caught on. "Breaks my heart to think I'm in competition for your affections, Miss Pearl."

Her cheeks reddened. "You are a silver-tongued devil. I see why Tiffany lost her senses around you. Take off your coat and let me whip some of these eggs into an omelet and pancakes."

"That sounds delicious, but how about I shovel the front and back walks while you cook. That's more of an even exchange."

"Deal. There's a snow shovel in the barn."

Rowdy found the shovel and made quick work of clearing the narrow path leading to the chicken coop. Around front, the wide brick walkway that led to the street took considerably longer, but that was okay. He wouldn't want Tiffany or her mom or grandmother risking a fall.

He'd known most of the Lawson women less than twenty-four hours yet already felt protective toward them. If he'd had his way, he and Tiffany would have already been hitched. Just because he needed her back in Virginia to watch after the baby didn't mean they couldn't also be friends.

TIFFANY WOKE TO too-bright sun streaming through her bedroom's tall, paned windows and the unnatural sound of metal scraping against rock. She winced before trying and failing to roll over and hide her ears beneath a pillow.

Mr. Bojangles peeked his head out from under his blanket.

She gave him a rub. "I know it's cold, but we need to find your booties and go outside. Want to change your sweater now or later?"

He ducked back under his cover.

She laughed. "We go through this every morning, sweetheart, but you know you will eventually have to leave this bed."

After three failed attempts to stand left Tiffany feeling like an upside-down roly-poly, she finally made it onto her feet but had to balance herself by grasping the back of the chaise.

"Baby, you are giving me quite a workout and it's not even eight." She gave her belly an affectionate rub before waddling to the window to draw back the lacy curtain.

Rowdy, in all his sheer male beauty, shoveled the front walk. The obnoxious clanging she'd heard had been the twang of his shovel hitting the brick pavers.

Tiffany groaned.

Part of her had been hoping his reentry into her life had been a dream.

He caught sight of her. Smiled and waved.

She dropped the curtain as if it had caught fire.

The other part of her? Oh—that part unfortunately felt like a giddy schoolgirl facing her first crush. His merest brush against her made her entire body hum. When he touched the baby bump they'd created, she lost the ability to think or even breathe. The man made her crave not pickles and ice cream but kisses and hugs and settling into a home with a family of her own. But the thing she had to remember was that she'd already had all of the above and it had vanished like a morning fog. Just like a sad country song, she'd lost her man, her house and her dignity.

At least she still had her dog.

Sort of.

Mr. Bojangles had taken a particular liking to Pearl—in no doubt due to her many handouts. If even her dog preferred other company to hers, what did that say for her mothering potential? As much as she adored the idea of becoming a mom to her son, the realities proved time and again that it was never meant to be.

She forced a deep breath, brushed hot tears from her cheeks with the back of her hand, then scooped Mr. Bojangles from the bed.

Whether he liked it or not, they both had to face the day. Which unfortunately also meant facing Rowdy.

"Please tell me that dog doesn't have his own red snow boots?" Rowdy leaned on the shovel's handle.

"Good morning to you, too." Tiffany set her pampered pup on the section of the walk he'd already shoveled. "Thank you for tackling this job. Usually I'm stuck doing it."

"But you're pregnant."

"Exactly. A few weeks back when we had that dusting, I figured it wouldn't be a big deal, but turns out it was. I was exhausted."

"One more reason to marry me for the sake of the baby. North Dakota isn't exactly known for balmy winters, yet my part of Virginia typically doesn't have it too bad."

She rolled her eyes before clutching the two halves of her inadequate wool coat as close as they'd go—not nearly all the way around her bulging tummy. He'd have to get her a new one. Maybe online? He couldn't let the mother of his child be cold.

"Look." Her sharp exhale clouded in the frosty air. "I appreciate you charging in here to act like my hero, but I'm perfectly capable of handling this situation on my own. There's not going to be a wedding, and right after ringing in the New Year—" she patted her belly "—our baby will be blissfully happy in his new home and you and I can get back to our separate lives as if none of this ever happened. Agreed?" She held out her hand for him to shake.

"Did you not hear a word I said last night? I'm not giving up on my son. Aren't you at least willing to try? Once you sign those papers, there's no going back. Can you honestly tell me you're that ready to give up a child that could be the best thing to ever happen to either of our lives?"

The dog left a yellow stain on the newly fallen snow.

Rowdy couldn't help but see it as a sign.

He cleared his throat. "Could you at least give me the courtesy of a reply?"

"It's cold. I need to get Mr. Bojangles inside." She scooped up her dog and left.

Rowdy took that as his cue to do the same.

He finished clearing the walk, returned the shovel to the barn, then trudged his way back to his truck. Since his words were clearly useless, he took his frustration with Tiffany out on the melting snow. Enough horsepower had gotten him out of a helluva lot of jams, and this time was no exception. The melting drift was no match for his dad's one-ton truck. As for this mess with Tiffany and his baby, looked like he'd need to rethink his strategy.

His specialty was brute force.

This situation called for a bit more finesse.

Meaning it was time to call in the big guns—his mother.

"MIGHT'VE BEEN NICE for you to let me know you were alive."

Rowdy entered his family home through the back door.

Patsy sat at the kitchen table. Judging by the array of paperwork spread around her, she was paying bills. Never the best time for a heart-to-heart.

"Sorry." He took off his boots before stepping onto her prized maple floor.

A welcoming fire crackled in the hearth, and sunshine added to the yellow room's already-cheery feel. So why did he still feel defeated?

"You'd better thank your lucky stars Pearl Lawson had the decency to let me know you were staying with her during the storm. I'd have called out the National Guard looking for you."

"Not to discount their great work, but I'm a SEAL. Think I could have survived a night in my truck." He rummaged in the fridge for sandwich fixings.

"Don't sass me. I'm already in a foul enough mood over your father's Visa bill. That man charged five hundred dollars' worth of fishing lures. How is that even possible? With the baby coming, we're going to need every spare dime to set up a nursery for when the baby stays here. I was thinking pale blue walls with an adorable cow-jumping-over-the-moon theme. What do you think?"

After opening the mayo, he sighed. "What I think is that unless you help me devise a plan to get Tiffany to change her mind about giving your grandson up for adoption, we could be in for one helluva fight."

"Oh, honey..." She put down the Visa bill

and removed her reading glasses. "What are you going to do?"

"I told her that for the sake of the baby, we should get married. Her mom and grandma seemed on board with the plan. Tiffany's the problem. She's got some fool notion that she's not fit to be a mom, but she babies her rat-sized dog like he's heir to the Lawson throne. Oh—and I guess money's a factor, but when I pointed out that I've got more than enough saved to provide a comfortable life for her and our baby, her pride kicks in and she starts spouting off about how she can do everything herself."

"Sweetheart, of course every woman is capable of supporting herself, but have you stopped to think about what that poor girl has been through? With her father in prison and her husband having left her, it's no wonder she's wary about jumping into another relationship."

He'd added mayo, shaved ham, lettuce and

pickles to the bread and now slapped a second piece of bread atop his creation.

"Didn't Pearl cook you a big country breakfast?"

"She offered, but Tiffany got me so riled I left before eating."

The back door opened, ushering in not only Rowdy's dad, James, but his big brother, Carl.

"Look what the cat dragged in," James said. "We sure could have used your help around here last night. That storm had cattle scattered all over hell and creation."

"Cut him some slack." Carl removed his long duster to hang it on the wall-mounted rack. He slapped his brown leather cowboy hat on the peg beside it. "Poor guy's had lady trouble. Justine said her friend Darcy, from Sunday school, told her that she knows a friend who plays bridge with the couple all set to adopt Tiffany's baby. They've been trying for years and couldn't be more pleased that they're getting a son."

"That's gotta be a special hell—" James sat on the entry bench to tug off his worn work boots "—to want a child and not be able to have one."

"No kidding, right? Lucky for us Jones men that we're nice and fertile."

James and Carl shared a laugh.

Rowdy didn't see a damned thing about his situation that was funny.

"Those people are *not* getting my son." Rowdy had held his sandwich to his mouth but now slapped it to the counter.

"Hon," Patsy said, "I've told you a million times to use a plate when you eat. You know I can't stand crumbs."

"Would you all listen to yourselves? This is my flesh and blood we're talking about. Yours, too. I'm all set to marry this woman, but she acts like my opinions don't even count. But I have rights. She can't just sign away my kid at her whim, can she?"

"I think the bigger question—" Carl helped himself to Rowdy's sandwich "—is what you are going to do with a kid. Have you set aside your own bullheaded pride long enough to consider the fact that Tiffany might be doing you a favor? I'm not saying this is by any means an easy decision, but it just might be the right one. This couple she's talking to seem like good people. They'll make equally good parents to some lucky kid—maybe even yours. Realistically, what do you have to offer?" He paused his rant to take another bite of Rowdy's sandwich. "A ratty apartment you share with four other guys. But that doesn't even matter when you're gone three hundred days out of the year. When you are home, you're on call or training. You're a full-fledged adrenaline junkie. How are you going to choose between sitting in the stands at your kid's fiftieth losing Little

League game versus planting explosives beneath some bad guy's ship? You think you're obligated to marry this woman, but take a good hard look at the bigger picture. Make no mistake, I love Justine and the girls, but I'd be lying if I said there are times I don't envy your path. But let's say you do convince Tiffany to marry your sorry ass? What then? What kind of life is that going to make for your son? Let alone his mom. What's she supposed to do with her days? Just sit around pining for you?"

"Your brother raises valid points," his dad said.

"Whose side are y'all on?" Rowdy hardened his jaw. "This is *my son* you're so casually talking about. All of our flesh and blood. Sure, I'll be first to admit changes will have to be made to my current way of life, but plenty of guys I serve with have kids and they all seem to do just fine."

"They're the exception," Patsy said. "Have

you seen the statistics on SEAL divorce rates? And those marriages started out with love. What you're proposing is more of a business arrangement."

"Stop." Rowdy pressed the heels of his hands against his closed eyes. With everything in him, he wanted to tell his family about what he'd been through with Brandi, but what would that do other than reinforce the fact that they were probably right—especially his mom with her divorce-rate statistics. He was a walking example of how easily a lonely woman found *entertainment*.

"Honey…" His mom left the table to give him a sideways hug. "No matter what you decide, we're all on Team Rowdy. If you're determined to see this through with Tiffany—make her your wife—just tell us how to help."

"That's just it," he said. "At this point, I'm not sure what to do. I proposed. She turned me down."

"Well, hell, son." Now his dad gave him a pat on his back. "You've got to woo her. And I'm talking a much deeper level than flowers and drugstore chocolates. You'll have to go all in. Really prove to this woman that you're husband and father material."

"How am I supposed to do that? I don't even have my own house."

Carl snorted. "Thought the navy was supposed to give him smarts. Tiffany's a Realtor, right? Kill two birds with one mortgage-sized stone. Have her show you every damned house in the county, then during all that time together, you can wow her with your charm."

"Duh. That was already my plan," Rowdy said with a put-upon sigh.

"For the record—" Patsy had left his side to take a pencil and notepad from the junk drawer, then get comfy on the window seat "—I think you're all wrong. Oh—I'm all for Rowdy showing Tiffany what a great catch he is, but in a roundabout way. Since you've already tried the direct approach and bombed, looks like you'll need to be sneakier. Now, I'm not usually in favor of playing games, but from what you've told me, this poor girl has been hurt to the point that she no longer takes a man's word at face value. What I want you to do is not *tell* her she's going to marry you but make her *ache* to marry you."

Rowdy frowned. "Mom, you might as well be speaking Martian. What does any of that mean?"

"Have a seat." She patted the cushion beside her. "I'll teach you everything I know…"

Chapter Six

"Grammy, what is this?" Two days after her last run-in with Rowdy, Tiffany had just come home after an endless day at the office to find a disturbing letter from the First Trust Bank lying on the desk she shared with her mom and grandmother.

Pearl snatched it from her hand. "Didn't your mother teach you it's not polite to snoop?"

"Please tell me this is a mistake?" The letter was a notice that Pearl was two months in arrears on paying her mortgage—a mortgage

Tiffany hadn't even known existed. "I thought Daddy paid off your house a long time ago?"

"He did, but then he needed cash for legal fees, and Tommy Peterson down at the bank was nice enough to help me fill out a few forms, and voilà—your father's legal fees were paid, so you and your mom didn't have to worry about them."

"But, Grammy, you now have to pay this bill every month. If you don't, that *nice* Tommy Peterson will take your house. You're already two payments behind. That's over a thousand dollars with late fees."

Her grandmother paled.

Which made Tiffany feel horrible for scolding one of the people she held most dear in the world. But she had enough on her plate with just paying utilities, car insurance, gasoline and grocery bills. How in the world would she ever manage an extra five hundred per month?

Thank goodness the Parkers were covering her obstetrician fees and prenatal vitamins.

"I'm sorry," Pearl said. "I figured we'd find the money somewhere."

Tiffany groaned, leaning forward in the desk chair. "We will, Grammy. Don't worry about it, okay? I'll figure something out."

"Of course you will. You've always been such a clever girl." Pearl kissed the crown of her head, then shuffled off toward the kitchen. "I'm making pork chops for dinner. Why don't you invite your handsome fiancé over for a nice hot meal?"

"Grammy, I already told you, Rowdy and I aren't getting married."

Pearl gave her a backhanded wave. "Sure you are, honey. You're carrying his baby. Maple Springs is a small town. If you don't marry him, tongues are going to wag."

"Grammy, no one cares about single women

having babies anymore. Besides, Susie and Jeb Parker are adopting the baby, remember?"

Why had she wasted her breath on the speech?

Pearl had already left the room, leaving Tiffany alone with too many worries and fears for one heart to bear.

"WAIT—PLEASE DON'T tell me you're Mr. *Gosee*?" Tiffany groaned before leaning back in her desk chair at Hearth and Home Realty. It had been a blessed whole week since she'd seen Rowdy. Halloween had come and gone, and she'd thought he'd returned to his submarine or ship or wherever it was navy SEALs spent their time.

"Right. Get it? As in I need to *go see* a few houses?" Rowdy flashed her that lopsided, toothy grin that got her all hot and bothered and wishing for a pitcher of margaritas and a dark dance floor on which she'd spend a few hours kissing him. All of which was stupid, considering as soon as their baby was born, odds were she'd never see him again. "I emailed all my needs. Do you have any properties lined up?"

"I did for your alter ego. But none for you."

"Aw, come on. My money spends just as good as his, and from what you've told me, you could use the commission."

"Of course I could, but do you have any idea how much trouble I'm in with Gigi and Pearl? I told them I have no intention of marrying you, and neither has spoken to me since. Even Mr. Bojangles is giving me the cold shoulder. He slept with Grammy last night."

"Can you blame him? Not only is she a great cook, but I like her sunny disposition. You're about as welcoming as barbed wire."

"I hate you."

"No, you don't."

"Oh—I really do." As if excited just hearing

his daddy's voice, her traitor baby kicked. "I have a plan. A good plan. You can't just come in here—"

"Whoa. Stop right there. I'm not here to discuss my son or our pending nuptials or anything other than buying a house. If you're not interested in making my home-ownership dreams a reality, then I'll ask your boss if he'd be willing to show me a few places." He stood.

"Sit down. If you promise to keep talk strictly on houses, I did find a few I think *Mr. Gosee* will like. But I'm warning you, if I get one hint that this is a trick and all you're really after is another shot at changing my mind about the adoption, I'll dump you right in the middle of the road—any road."

"Fair enough." He offered her his hand to shake.

After eyeing his outstretched hand with a narrow-eyed glare, she turned her attention to her computer, printing fact sheets for three small ranches. "Per *Mr. Gosee's* request, these are all horse properties. One has a full barn—the others have rustic lean-tos that could, of course, be improved." She handed him the papers, then retrieved her purse and three mini Snickers bars from her bottom drawer. Since tequila was off the table as a stress reliever, chocolate would have to do.

Keys jingling, she squeezed into her coat, then led the way from her office, all too conscious of his presence. He made her feel hot and tingly and hyperaware. The last place she wanted him was behind her, but if he'd been in front, then she'd have been tortured by the view of his backside hugged by faded Wranglers.

"Would you rather I drive?" he asked when she struggled to fit behind the wheel.

"I can manage."

"I don't doubt you can, but what would it

hurt for you to kick back and let me serve as your chauffeur?"

His offer was tempting…

It was only ten thirty, yet her lower back throbbed. Don't get her started on how her swollen feet had turned numb from being squeezed into heels.

"You forget, I grew up around here and know all the best shortcuts."

"Okay." She handed over her keys and they made the seating transition. "But no funny business. We're strictly house-hunting. That's all."

"You have my solemn vow."

She snorted. "Seems like you gave me that the night I got pregnant. Let's see… How did that go?" She lowered her voice to mock him. "'Baby, I give you my solemn vow as a bull rider that you'll never have another ride any-where near as fine as this.'" She tried folding her arms, but her sleeves were mortifyingly too tight to allow for the simple movement, so she settled for glaring out the passenger-side window. "Have you ever even ridden a bull?"

"That hurts." He clutched his chest before backing out of her assigned space in the lot behind the office. "I'll have you know I was almost state champion back in— Well, let me think about it. It was three years before I graduated high school, so that would've been—"

"Never mind." She glared harder.

"Turnabout's fair play. You told me you were a rodeo queen. Is that true?"

"Absolutely. I've won several titles."

"Name one."

"Name one of yours."

"I asked you first."

"So you weren't a rodeo queen?"

"So you weren't a bull-riding champion?"

At a stop sign, he slanted a breathtaking grin in her direction and she lost it. She laughed and he laughed and then pregnancy hormones had her crying from the absurdity of their situation.

"Truth—" she dabbed the corners of her eyes with a tissue she'd taken from her purse "—I was fourth runner-up in the Miss Rodeo Fort Worth competition when I was sixteen. But a horrible girl named Windy—spelled with an *i*—*accidentally* spilled nachos down the front of my custom-made white satin pantsuit. If it hadn't been for her, I have no doubt I would have worn the crown."

"Hell, yeah, you would have." At a four-way stop, he fixed her with a look so intense, so downright mesmerizing, her heart skipped a beat. "You're gorgeous."

"You're sweet." Pulse on a treacherous gallop, she looked at her hands clasped atop their baby. How long had it been since a man told her she was pretty? A while. Not since she and Rowdy had first been together. "She was a far better barrel racer. Even without the sabotage, she probably would have won."

"Don't sell yourself short. A lot of women might have fallen apart after what you've been through, but adversity seems to have made you stronger."

His kind words were hot chocolate. A crackling fire. A foot massage followed by—

From behind them a FedEx driver honked.

"Sorry," he said along with a backward courtesy wave. "To him—not to you."

They rode the rest of the way to the first house in silence, but something about his compliment warmed her on a fundamental level. She had fought for so long—for *everything*. Not just for money to pay bills, but to keep her mother and grandmother comfortable. To eat healthy and care for the miracle growing inside her that she would all too soon gift to a more deserving mother.

Truth be told, she didn't used to be a nice

person. Maybe she hadn't loved Crawford the way she should have? Maybe if she'd been more focused on his needs instead of planning what to wear to her next charity event, he might have stood by her side when her dad's business had taken such an ugly fall?

"This it?" His question provided a welcome respite from her dark thoughts.

Since she could no longer afford her smartphone, she eyed her county map. "Looks like it. The home is vacant, so pull right into the drive."

Though the main roads were clear, patches of slushy snow made the trek down the dirt drive less than ideal.

"I apologize for this. The owner's out of state. I should have thought to have it plowed."

"No worries. I'll park in a dry patch so you don't ruin those fancy shoes."

"Thanks." He noticed? Rowdy was full of all kinds of surprises this morning.

The two-story classic American bungalow featured a wide front porch supported by sturdy square columns. But the place was in need of a thorough cleaning, as brown leaves and a thick coating of dust covered the wood-plank porch floor.

Tiffany fumbled with the lockbox but eventually led them into the dark home. "It's a total fixer-upper, but with a price of fifty thousand, you'd have plenty of room in your budget to renovate. There are four bedrooms. One full bathroom to share upstairs and a powder room on the ground floor for guests."

The carpet was gold '70s shag and birds could be heard chattering in the chimney. Heavy gold velvet drapes were drawn and mildew was the prevailing scent in the air. Water stains marred the sagging ceiling.

"There's probably hardwood under the carpet. Want me to tug back a corner so you can take a look?"

"Thanks for the offer, but I'm getting serious haunted vibes from this place. Let's check out the next place on our list."

"Are you sure? We haven't even seen the kitchen. Plus, there are ten acres of good grazing land for your horse."

"Thanks, but no thanks. I mean, come on. At any price, could you see yourself living here?"

"Rowdy…" she warned. "You promised your sudden drive to become a homeowner had nothing to do with me."

"It doesn't. It was a rhetorical question."

"Oh—well, in that case, no. This place gives me the creeps."

Tiffany locked up the house and had never been more relieved to be back in a car—any car. Not because she'd been that afraid of the spooky old house but because her feet seriously hurt. What had she been thinking? Heels and her seventh month of pregnancy had been an awful idea.

Upon reaching the end of the drive, Rowdy took a left. "The info sheet says this next house has a hot tub. I'm excited to see that."

She leaned her head back and closed her eyes. "Hate to be a party pooper, but don't hold your breath. I can't count the number of listings I get all jacked up to see, then they wind up being an agent's work of fiction. Like this one time, I saw that a listing featured an atrium. My client had been transferred here from Jacksonville, Florida, and missed her sunshine. Well, that was before I learned to preview properties, and boy, did we get a surprise. That sun-flooded atrium we envisioned to be glass walled with palm trees and parrots? Turned out to be a hallway that had a leaky ceiling. The owner's solution had been to bust the roof all the way out, staple tarps to the edges, and sledgehammer holes in the walls of other rooms that they then used for a new hall. It was bizarre."

Rowdy whistled. "Gotta give 'em points for creativity."

He punched the new address into his phone, then set the route. "What did you do before selling homes?"

"I'm kind of embarrassed to say, but nothing."

"You had to do something."

She shrugged. "I lunched. Shopped. Did charity work."

"See? Charity's a good thing."

"I suppose."

"Why do you sound so down? As my Realtor, aren't you supposed to be chatting me up?"

"Sorry." She forced a smile. "Something occurred to me, and I haven't been able to get the thought from my mind."

"Lay it on me." He turned onto Ponderosa Court.

"Remember what you said earlier? About adversity having made me stronger?"

"Sure. What about it?"

"When Brandi did what she did—you know, sleeping around on you—did you feel guilty?"

"No way. Why should I feel bad because of what she did? But what does any of what I went through have to do with you?"

"Nothing." She shook her head, aiming the heater vent down from her flushed face. "At least not directly. But part of me wonders if I had been a better wife, maybe Crawford would have stood by my side through Daddy's troubles."

"Back up the truck." He cast her a sideways glance. "You don't really believe that, do you? That somehow you're to blame for your idiot husband leaving you when you needed him most? That's BS. I'm assuming you two went with the traditional vows, meaning he was aware of the whole for-better-or-worse scenario? Plus, he was hitched to you—not your father."

"You make it sound so black-and-white."

"It is. A man doesn't leave a woman when she's down—at least not me. I wasn't raised that way."

"Remember when you wanted me to meet your mom?"

"Sure. Want to come for dinner some night? Or we could just stick with the original offer of cinnamon rolls."

"That sounds nice, but…" Suddenly emotional for no reason, Tiffany wanted to say yes but shook her head. Getting close to Rowdy's family would only make her decision more painful for all involved. Before now, she hadn't considered the fact that it wasn't just Rowdy whose life would be impacted by her giving up the baby. Though his big brother had already given his parents two granddaughters, did they want more? Obviously, they must be proud of their hotshot SEAL son, but did they want more for him? A daughter-in-law and more grandchildren and for him to settle down closer to their family home? "Definitely no."

"Why not? Mom and Dad are great. You'd like them."

"I'm sure I would." Which was the problem. The bigger her baby grew, the closer she came to her heart officially breaking when it was time to hand him over to the Parkers. She couldn't then turn around and do that to Rowdy's family, too.

"Then why not come for dinner?"

"Rowdy…" She sighed.

He held up his hands. "Invitation rescinded."

"Thanks." It crushed her that he gave up so easily, but then, why had she expected anything different when she'd asked to keep their dealings on a professional level?

They arrived at the next house.

This one was an A-frame overlooking a four-acre lake. Though the home had been painted an unfortunate shade of electric blue, the landscaping was lovely. Rolling hills dotted with patches of forest and snow-covered pasture.

"Hope this comes with a riding mower." Out of the car, Rowdy held his hand to his forehead, shading his eyes from the sun.

"Why would you need to mow anything? Can't your horse eat the grass?"

"See those fences?" He pointed to newish-looking split-rail fences rimming the property. "Since it says on the info sheet that this has thirty-six acres, it stands to reason that the area not fenced is what they consider a lawn. I'm a fairly good judge of distance, and I'm going to say that's about three football fields' worth of lawn my wife is going to want me to mow every Saturday afternoon when I'd rather be watching college football."

"But you're not married." Her chest squeezed uncomfortably at the thought of him one day living here—or anywhere—with another woman. What was the significance of the fact that she didn't want him but she sure didn't want him canoodling with anyone else?

"For now, I'm single. But I'm a great catch. Out on the open market, I won't last long."

She rolled her eyes.

He winked.

Butterflies fluttered in her tummy.

"Buying a house is a big commitment," Rowdy said. "Eventually, when I retire from the navy, I'll end up back here, helping my dad and brother. Whoever I marry will have to get along with my mom and Justine. I assume they'll go shopping and garden and bake together. Plus, they do charity work."

On the meandering path to the home's front door, Tiffany asked, "What sorts of charities? In Dallas I volunteered for the local animal shelter."

"Nice. I think Mom works at the hospital—showing visitors to patient rooms, delivering flowers, that kind of stuff. Justine reads books to old folks at Pine Manor. It's a retirement center."

"They sound like sweethearts."

"They are."

For some unfathomable reason, her hands shook while trying to work the combination on the lockbox. What would Rowdy's mom and sister-in-law think about her giving her son up for adoption? As mothers, would they look down on her? Or understand?

Most days, Tiffany didn't even understand.

But she felt backed into a corner.

Not only did she not feel emotionally strong enough to be a good mother, but the whole financial strain seemed insurmountable. She truly had no other option.

What about Rowdy? her conscience nudged. *How many times has he proposed?*

Funny, but accepting his offer of marriage struck her as a cop-out. The coward's solution to her problems. He hadn't gotten her into this money mess. How would it then be fair to expect his help? They were virtual strangers. Aside from their lone hot night, they had nothing in common. Sure, the baby was half his responsibility, but the last thing she wanted was for him to feel trapped like he had with Brandi.

Most important, Tiffany deserved more than what would essentially be a marriage of convenience. *If* she ever married again, it would be forever. Rowdy was sweet, but not exactly a forever kind of guy.

"Need help?"

She looked up to find him kneeling alongside her.

His face was close enough to hers that with minimum effort, she could have leaned forward to press her lips to his. She could have. And it was an undeniable fact that kissing him would feel beyond amazing. *Sublime.* But what would that solve? There was no denying their physical chemistry. But that had nothing to do with the kind of love it took to sustain a forever kind of marriage.

"Tiff?" He cleared his throat. "You okay?"

Free hand to her throat, she hastily nodded.

"You look pale. Need a break?"

"No. I'm good. Great." The lockbox popped and the house keys dropped into her open palm. "Okay, we're in."

She opened the door to enter a space that more closely resembled a taxidermy shop than living room.

"Hmm…" Rowdy arched his head back, taking it all in. The area featured an at-least-twenty-five-foot vaulted ceiling. Every inch of available wall space was covered in heads—deer, antelope, elk, bighorn sheep. An eight-foot grizzly stood in a corner. The air felt oppressive from the creatures' ghosts. "I guess this beats my roommate's centerfold pics."

"Look beyond the current decor. Remember, all of this will be going along with the owners."

"And their plaid furniture? Never been a fan of plaid."

"What if your wife loves it?"

"She won't."

"How do you know?"

"It's a deal breaker. If we get to the stage in our relationship where I'm thinking of popping the question, then I'll first ask about her relationship with plaid."

Tiffany rolled her eyes. "If you'll follow me upstairs, we'll look at the bedrooms."

"I've seen enough. We can move on."

"But don't you at least want to see the kitchen? And what about the hot tub?" She pointed toward the sliding glass windows leading to the deck.

"I'm good. I'll know the right place when I see it, and sorry, but this isn't it."

Tiffany sighed.

In her perfect dream scenario, *Mr. Gosee* would have fallen for the very first house they'd toured. The more she was forced to be with Rowdy, the more curious she grew about the type of woman he would one day be with. Beyond a physical type, what personality traits would he find irresistible? A sense of humor? Intellect? Was he looking for a great conversationalist or lover?

She shouldn't care but oddly did.

Her cheeks heated at the realization that she already knew what qualities he appreciated in the bedroom. The sex between them had been—

"Tiff, holy crap." He pointed at her feet. "Why didn't you tell me you need a break?"

"Huh?" She'd been so deep in thought about her baby's father that she'd forgotten her own rule about their house-seeking mission being strictly platonic. "What do you mean? We still have another house to see."

"You're not going anywhere but home. You have to get off of those footballs you call feet."

She glanced down to find that her feet and ankles had swollen to the point that the skin beneath her nude pantyhose had reddened. She hadn't felt any pain, because they'd gone past that point to numb.

Fear slithered through her in disorientating waves. "I've read about this in books. Do you think something's wrong with the baby?"

"There's only one way to find out. We're taking you to the ER." Before she could even think about launching a protest, he scooped her into his arms.

Chapter Seven

Our baby.

While the doctor examined Tiffany, Rowdy paced in the ER's crowded waiting area. A TV blared some god-awful kid show and an assortment of moans, coughs and general conversations interfered with the signal usually telling his brain to chill during emergencies.

But that was when bad guys shot at him.

This was a whole nother ball game.

He'd gladly take a bullet over the emotional strain of wondering what was going on behind closed exam room doors. He'd been seated in the hard plastic chair for two freakin' hours. What could be taking so long? Should he call Tiffany's mom and grandmother? Should he call his parents? What was the protocol on this situation? He needed a manual. At the very least, an officer barking orders.

But if he was on the verge of becoming a father, what did that say about his parenting skills? When it came to any family emergency, his mom and dad always seemed to know exactly what to do. What was wrong with him that he didn't?

And what was happening with the hospital bill? As the baby's father, shouldn't someone have asked him about insurance? He assumed his military coverage would automatically include his unborn child, but that was another issue he'd need to look into.

A pinched voice said over an intercom, "Mr. Jones, please come to the service desk."

Rowdy stood, but then so did an elderly man dressed in overalls and a red shirt. His green ball cap read McGinty's Tack and Feed.

They reached the desk at about the same time.

In deference to the man's age, Rowdy gestured for him to approach the clerk first. He wanted to think the kindness was because his folks raised him right, but the God's honest truth was that he wasn't sure he was ready to handle bad news should something be wrong with Tiffany or their baby.

Turned out the older gentleman had been the Mr. Jones in question, so Rowdy started to sit back down, but his seat had been taken by a teen boy with a nose ring and green hair. If that were his kid, he'd shave him bald and yank the ring out with pliers.

But then, hell. What kind of parent didn't allow their child to experiment with his or her personal sense of style? The summer between his junior and senior years of high school, he'd gone through his own brief Goth stage. His folks hadn't much liked it, but they hadn't stopped him.

Could Tiffany be right? Could neither one of them be ready to be parents to this baby who was barreling their way?

He paced in front of the snack machines for a good thirty minutes before hearing his name again called over the intercom. This time an orderly greeted him and led him to the curtained-off room where Tiffany and her enormous belly sat up on a too-narrow bed. Her complexion had turned sallow, her formerly tidy bun had fallen and she'd sucked her lower lip into her mouth as if trying with all her might not to cry.

"Babe, what's wrong?" he asked at her side, forgetting his mother's order not to show how much he actually cared.

"I have edema and my blood pressure's too

high. The doctor put me on bed rest for the week. But I have showings scheduled for three clients. I can't just lounge in bed. Mom and Grammy need the money from those potential sales."

"Slow down…" He took her hand, giving her a gentle squeeze. "Right now all that matters is keeping you and the baby healthy. Everything else can wait."

She shook her head. "If I don't get those commissions, who knows what could happen? Grammy could lose her house. She didn't want anyone to know, but I found out by accident that she mortgaged it to pay off Dad's legal fees." Her heart rate skyrocketed on the monitor, as did the baby's.

"Relax…" Rowdy coached. "Take a few deep breaths. It takes a long time for a bank to officially foreclose. One of my idiot roommates, Connor, bought a great condo he was going to fix up on weekends and sell for a nice profit, but then we got deployed. He thought he'd set up auto-payments but never went to the bank to sign the forms. Long story short—he didn't make his payment for six months, but once he got back, he got it all sorted out and he eventually made a killing. If it makes you feel better, I'll go show the houses on your behalf."

"If only that would be legal. But if it were, you'd do that?" She met his gaze and the intensity of their connection caused his pulse to race as fast as hers. Didn't she know by now that he'd do anything for her and their unborn child? But why? He barely knew her yet couldn't shake the sensation that he'd always known her. That he couldn't imagine life without her. Not a good thing considering maybe she'd been right about the adoption all along.

"Sure." He strove for a light tone. Like she hadn't turned his entire world upside down and inside out and every damned way in between.

She sharply exhaled. "That would've been great. Thanks for the offer."

"No problem."

A man and woman suddenly rushed into the room. "Thank goodness you're okay."

Rowdy glanced over his shoulder to find the sort of power couple he'd seen only on TV. The man with slicked-back blond hair wore a navy suit, pin-striped shirt and red power tie. The set of his mouth was pinched with worry. The woman with him had sleek dark hair. A red dress with black stockings and heels. More gold around her neck, wrists and fingers than Fort Knox. Yet her bloodshot eyes looked as if she'd been crying. She clenched a tissue in her hand.

Let me guess—Jeb and Susie Parker? His son's adoptive parents.

No wonder no emergency room staff had asked him about payment. When Tiffany called in the cavalry, they'd probably made all the necessary arrangements for the bill to be paid.

Rowdy wanted to hate them but felt an odd compassion for this couple who for all outward appearances seemed to have everything yet lacked the ability to conceive their own child.

"Tiffany…" The woman dabbed the corners of her eyes with a tissue. "We got your call and I swear I haven't breathed since. But the doctor said you and the baby will be all right? You just need rest?"

Tiffany nodded. Her gaze darted from him to the couple. "Susie, Jeb—this is Rowdy. He's the baby's biological father."

"Oh." Susie looked from Tiffany to Rowdy, then raised her trembling hands to her mouth. "Oh, God…" She shook her head, then turned to her husband, hiding her face against his pricey suit's lapel. Suddenly, they were no longer powerful and all the money in the world meant nothing compared to the gift of a new-born son they believed they were receiving.

"Shh…" Jeb said to his wife. "Don't jump to conclusions." He held out his hand to Rowdy, forcing a tight smile. "Nice to meet you. We, ah, can't thank you enough for your remark-able sacrifice."

About that…

"Yeah. Sure." Rowdy shook the guy's hand but then felt so overcome by raw emotion that he cleared his throat, then said, "I'll leave you all alone. Tiff, I'm guessing you'll want the Parkers to drive you home?"

Her eyes also shone with tears. She opened her mouth to speak but then clamped her lips shut and merely nodded.

Rowdy's heart felt near exploding from pain and confusion, so he left.

He should have stayed.

He should have told this couple here and now that there was no way in hell they'd ever be raising *his* son. But how could he claim any of that when he'd never been more confused?

After driving aimlessly for thirty minutes in Tiffany's SUV, knowing he'd have to at least see her again to return her vehicle, he wound up back at his family's ranch.

The day had turned into the perfect Indian-summer afternoon. After the early snow, what few leaves remained on the oaks and maples surrounding the house and barn were putting on a colorful show.

While parking Tiffany's SUV—his truck was back at her office—Rowdy spotted his brother teaching a gelding, Dandy, manners in the round pen, so he sauntered that way, appreciating the scents of loamy soil and hay.

"You look like hell," Carl said. He gave the black gelding a rub, then led him out the gate to play. The last time Rowdy had been in, the gelding had been a little guy. Now he was almost ready for saddling. He missed a lot being gone from the ranch. But he loved serving his country.

He loved being a SEAL.

His job wasn't merely a paycheck but his calling.

Rowdy said, "Feel like it, too."

"What's up?"

Where did he start? Why hadn't he told the Parkers that his son would never be theirs? "You're a dad—a great one."

"Yeah. What about it?" Carl aimed for the barn.

Rowdy climbed over the fence to meet him inside. It took his eyes time to adjust to the shadows. He'd always felt at peace in the quiet barn. In a way, it was his church—slanted sunbeams filled with dust motes his dad used to tell him were angels, watching over him and keeping him safe. The rich aroma of leather tack that had been in the family for generations, lovingly cared for and oiled, made him feel a profoundly deep connection to not only his family but the land.

Carl said, "Prying words out of you is about as easy as it's been getting Dandy prepped for saddling." He took a pair of well-worn leather gloves from a shelf and handed them to him. "If you can't tell me what's wrong, at least make yourself useful. The stalls all need cleaning. Ingrid has an ear infection, so I had to run her to the pediatrician this morning instead of doing my usual chores."

"Where's Dad?"

"South pasture. He found a calf with scours, so he's bringing him in for treatment."

Rowdy nodded.

Carl handed him a pitchfork, then took a wheelbarrow down to the last stall. This time of year, they brought most of the horses in for the night. Though cattle were the ranch's biggest source of income, they also raised and trained horses. Carl and his father had earned the reputation of being a couple of the best trainers around.

What was Rowdy good at? Sniffing trouble.

His nickname with his buddies was Voodoo because he had an uncanny knack for exposing the earth's human scum. This ability came in real handy while on active duty in Iraq or Afghanistan, but it wouldn't do beans for him in North Dakota.

One more reason to reconsider becoming a father?

His chest ached from the decision rocketing toward him faster than enemy fire. By his calculations, Tiffany had about six weeks until she delivered their son. In that time, he'd have to make what now struck him as an impossible choice.

Together, Rowdy and Carl cleaned three stalls without saying a word.

But then Rowdy's dam of silence broke. "I was out with Tiffany this afternoon, looking at houses like y'all told me to, when I noticed her feet looked like a pair of footballs."

"It happens. With both pregnancies, Justine had to spend a lot of time off her feet. She teased that was nature's way of telling me to spoil her rotten." He smiled. "Damn, I love that woman."

In the moment, Rowdy envied his big brother and his friend Duck. Both of them seemed to have life figured out.

"Did you take her to her doctor?"

"Her feet were so big I ran her straight to the ER. Long story short, you're right. The doc told her to stay off her feet for the next few days. Oh—and she needs to stop cramming her toes into silly high heels."

"Sounds like a solid plan. So what's the problem?"

Rowdy shoveled faster. "While we were at the hospital, this frantic couple stormed into

Tiff's room. Turns out they're the adoptive parents she selected."

Carl whistled. "Bet that was an ugly scene. How'd they take the news that your son is no longer on the market?"

"That's just it." Rowdy froze, resting his hands atop the pitchfork. "I couldn't tell them. The woman—Susie—was crying with worry over the baby. Her husband, Jeb, was a real professional type. Suit. Tie. The whole nine yards. But even he had tears in his eyes. And I stood there looking at them, thinking they already love my son. They have loved him longer than I've even known he existed. They probably have a nursery already in place and, hell, a preschool application at some fancy-ass academy where rich folks send their kids to get trained to be even richer. But what do I have to offer? Like Mom pointed out, the vast majority of the year, I'm not even in the country. Can you imagine being away from Isobel and Ingrid for that long?"

"Honestly? No."

"See? So what if I was wrong to head up here, demanding Tiffany and I force a marriage when neither one of us are anywhere near ready to settle down? We don't know the first thing about raising a baby. Hell, what do I know about changing diapers or making formula? I like to think someday I'd make a good dad, but how do I know now is that time?"

"You know when you know."

"What's that mean?"

"Just what I said. Look, when Justine first told me she was pregnant with Izzy—not gonna lie, I was scared shitless. But that's why the good Lord saw fit to give us nine months to get used to the idea. So that by the time the baby enters the world, you've got yourself good and psyched up. Then, once you see him or her..." his eyes welled and he tapped the center of his chest "...it's magic. Indescribable. You just know that suddenly the most important person in your world is this tiny, squalling, red-faced creature who holds your heart in her tiny hands. Or, in your case, his hands." He sighed. "I'm not passing judgment. If you don't feel like now is the time for you to be a dad, I can't say I understand, but I'm not going to love you any less. I'm sure as hell not going to judge—neither are Mom and Dad. Only you can decide if you're ready to be a father. And if Tiffany maintains that she can't handle custody, then it might come down to you having to raise this baby boy on your own. Not sure how you'd do that while deployed, but we're a family and we'd figure it out."

Rowdy wished his big brother's sage words made him feel better, but if anything, he'd only grown more confused.

Chapter Eight

"How exciting," Pearl said not thirty seconds after Tiffany and the Parkers entered the house. "It's rare to have company around here, and you all make for three in the same week. How do you know our Tiffany?"

"Grammy, these are the baby's adoptive parents." Tiffany made formal introductions. "I had a problem with swollen feet this afternoon, so Rowdy took me to the ER. Jeb and Susie were kind enough to give me a ride home. I guess Rowdy will stop by later with my car."

"Gracious." Hand to her chest, Pearl made a clucking sound. "Hope it's nothing serious?"

Mr. Bojangles danced at Susie's and Jeb's feet. He wasn't wearing the black sweater she'd put on him that morning. Was he cold?

Gigi wandered in, fluffing her hair. "Why didn't anyone tell me we have guests? I would have done something with myself." Of course, Gigi looked flawless in full makeup, curled hair and a flowing, bejeweled caftan far more suited to Dubai than North Dakota.

"Hush." Pearl landed a light swat to her daughter-in-law's shoulder. "Tiffany's sick, and these are the people who will be taking her baby."

"But I thought she was marrying Rowdy and keeping the baby? I've been on the phone with florists and caterers most of the afternoon."

Poor Susie paled.

Jeb wrapped his arm around her shoulders as support.

For some unfathomable reason, Tiffany wished for Rowdy to give her the same comforting treatment, but that train had long left the station. Judging by the dark look he'd sported while meeting their son's adoptive parents, he'd been as shocked to see them as they had been upon meeting him.

Susie's eyes teared, but she managed to say, "We were under the impression the baby's father was no longer in the picture?"

"He wasn't. He's not," Tiffany assured them. The drive over, Susie had been on the phone with a private nursing company. Despite Tiffany's protests, she'd been determined to provide round-the-clock care.

"That's not what he told us," Pearl stated. "That man declared his intentions, so I'm real sorry," she said to Susie and Jeb, "but Tiffany and Rowdy will be keeping their baby."

"Don't listen to them." For the baby, Tiffany needed to get this issue behind her and sit down. Her feet were already once again starting to swell. "Susie, Jeb, I know the baby's father showing up has put a slight kink in our plans, but I wholeheartedly believe he'll come around. Please, for now, I can't thank you enough for charging to my rescue, but I need rest."

"What about the private nurses?" Jeb asked.

Pearl raised her chin. "I might be old, but I'm plenty capable of caring for my own grand-child."

As if sensing the tension, Mr. Bojangles barked.

"Grammy—" Tiffany awkwardly knelt to pick up her anxious dog "—the doctor told me I need to be on bed rest for the week. I can't burden you with that."

"Nonsense. I—"

A brief knock sounded on the still-ajar front door. Then Rowdy stepped into the fray. "If anyone's going to care for Tiffany and our baby, it'll be me."

Once again Tiffany nearly swooned.

She scolded her stupid, romantic heart. The only service Rowdy currently performed was acting as one more person wanting something from her that she wasn't equipped to give.

"So that's it?" Jeb asked. "Man-to-man, you're not willing to sign away your parental rights?"

"Honestly?" Rowdy's whisker-stubbled jaw hardened and he shoved his hands in his jeans pockets. "I'm not sure. I'd be lying if I said I wasn't leaning in that direction, but my military career isn't exactly family friendly, so that's got me wondering if maybe an adoption would be best?"

Susie took a tissue from her purse and blotted her watery eyes. Tiffany's heart ached for the poor woman. She'd been trying to get pregnant for nearly a decade. Wanting a baby consumed her. To now snatch back this most precious gift would be beyond cruel.

"We'll need a definitive answer," Jeb said. "My wife is a strong woman, but—"

"I can speak for myself," Susie said. "Rowdy, Tiffany explained how you only just recently found out you were going to be a father, so I'm sure you're still adjusting to the news. Please know that if you were to decide to go through with the adoption, we'd be forever in your debt. Your son would never want for love or anything else."

"I appreciate that," Rowdy said, "but you've got to understand that this decision is going to take a minute."

"Of course." She bowed her head.

"If I did decide to sign over my parental rights, would I at least be involved in my child's life? Or are we talking about a closed adoption?"

"Closed," Jeb said. "Sorry, but I think it's

best for the child to believe we're his parents in every sense of the word. Someday down the line—maybe when he's in college, we could tell him the truth, but—"

"I get it." Rowdy held up his hands to stop Jeb's speech.

"What about the wedding?" Gigi asked.

"Mom, please, stay out of this. And for the last time, there's not going to be a…" Suddenly light-headed, Tiffany grasped the newel post for support.

"This party's over," Rowdy said, already by her side, scooping her into his arms. "Jeb, Susie, we'll let you know when we have an answer. Until then, please respect the fact that this isn't an easy choice for any of us. We'll let you know what we've decided as soon as we know."

He carried her up the stairs, tenderly deposited her on the bed, then took the dog from her to set him atop her towering belly, where he served as king of the mountain.

She didn't have the energy to move him.

It was only a little past five, but the afternoon had been beyond exhausting.

To the dog, Rowdy said, "Watch over your mom and my son, okay? I'll be right back."

"Where are you going?" Tiffany asked.

"To finish a conversation." He removed her heels, then pitched them across the room. He took her favorite fuzzy blanket from the foot of the bed, lifted Mr. Bojangles long enough to cover her, then set the dog back on her belly while adjusting her pillows. "Comfortable?"

She nodded.

"I'll be back with food and something to drink. Don't you dare move a muscle. Are we clear?"

"Yes, sir." She made a sassy salute.

Her SEAL growled before storming out her bedroom door, closing it behind him.

She closed her eyes and tried sleeping, but that was kind of tough considering the raised voices floating up the stairs. Not to mention the fact that she'd just thought of Rowdy in terms of being *hers*, when nothing could be further from the truth.

ROWDY DESCENDED THE stairs to find himself immersed in the sort of verbal ugliness he hadn't seen since his last visit to Mogadishu.

Jeb fought with Pearl.

Susie warred with Gigi.

What all of them had forgotten was that upstairs, the woman carrying the unborn child they bickered over was in less-than-ideal health. Tiffany needed care and support—not infighting over custody of a child who would rightfully be his.

Sick of the noise, he put his fingers in his mouth for an ear-piercing whistle. When all four of them stopped yammering to stare, he said, "Susie and Jeb, I appreciate your help." He fished one of his family ranch business cards from his wallet to hand to Jeb. "Whatever the medical costs turn out to be, please forward them to me at this address."

"This isn't about money," Susie said. "We want your baby."

"I get that. Your message has come through loud and clear. But right now my sole focus is Tiffany. She needs peace and quiet. Which means you two need to leave."

"I thought you said you just needed time. D-does this mean you've already made a decision?" Tears streamed down Susie's cheeks.

"I honestly don't know. At the moment, all I do know is that like I already told you, the best I can offer is to give you a decision closer to when the baby's due. Until then, I'd appreciate not seeing either of you again."

"We do have rights," Jeb noted. "The adoption will be legal just as soon as Tiffany signs a contract."

"Yeah…" He opened the front door and gestured the way out. "Well, that was before I was in the picture. Now that I'm back in, you can take your contract and shove it up your—"

"I think they get the message," Pearl said with a calming hand to his back. "Susie and Jeb, I'm sure Tiffany will call should her condition change."

"You'll be hearing from my lawyer," Jeb said before ushering a sobbing Susie out the door.

Once they'd left, Rowdy leaned hard against the nearest wall, closing his eyes for a moment to drag in an extra-deep breath.

"I had no idea you were such a powerful orator," Gigi said. "Perhaps at the wedding, you and Tiffany should write your own vows?"

If a guy like Jeb had said that, Rowdy probably would have decked him for the ridiculous comment, but Tiffany's mother looked so sincere all he could do was laugh. "If it comes to that, we'll see. But for now, could one of you please help me make Tiff a cup of herbal tea?"

"It would be my most sincere pleasure," Pearl said. "I have fresh-baked oatmeal cookies, too. I always add a smidge more vanilla than the recipe calls for. Makes them extra tasty."

"I can't wait to find out." Rowdy followed both women to the kitchen, where Gigi chattered about the holiday-themed wedding that was never going to happen. Meanwhile, Pearl prepared a tray loaded with three small baskets of cookies, muffins and grapes. Once the teakettle whistled on the gas stove, she poured steaming water over the tea bag she'd already placed in a dainty floral cup.

"Here you go," she said once she'd finished. "Need help delivering it to our patient?"

"No, thank you. You've done enough by putting all this together."

His simple praise left the kindly old woman beaming.

Gigi sported a huge smile, too. "Mother Lawson, it sure is nice having a man around the house, isn't it?"

"Yes, ma'am, it sure is. I'm excited for the wedding. I might tackle the cake all on my own."

"You do make beautiful cakes." Gigi snatched a cookie from her daughter's tray.

Rowdy didn't have the heart to tell them the wedding was a figment of their imaginations, so he retreated up the rambling farmhouse's back stairs.

It was tricky cradling the tray in the crook of one arm while turning the crystal doorknob to Tiffany's room, but once he was in, the sight awaiting him took his breath away.

Tiffany and her sorry excuse for a guard dog had fallen asleep. Both lightly snored, and both were bathed in the setting sun's golden glow.

She was a beauty.

He recalled the night they'd met like it had happened eight minutes earlier as opposed to eight months.

How had all of this gotten so messy?

When he'd learned of her pregnancy, he'd planned for a simple extraction mission. Pick up the woman carrying his baby, bring her back to Virginia, set her up in a house. Problem solved, right? But somewhere along the way, she'd gotten under his skin. He found himself wanting to do little things for her. Hefting her into his arms more because he craved holding her rather than because she wasn't able to walk.

Swiping his hands through his hair, he tried looking at this cluster bomb of a situation with a clinical view.

But a pang in his chest stopped all signals from going to his brain. Where his logic used to live now resided an unfamiliar craving for a more elusive something he couldn't wholly identify, let alone find.

His every current problem stemmed from this woman.

Her blond hair streamed across the pillow, catching glints from the sun as if she were his own personal siren. In that moment, he didn't want to be with her for the sake of the baby, but because he wanted to kiss her.

For a guy whose tightest relationship was with the US Navy? Craving a woman was a very bad thing.

Chapter Nine

It was just her luck that when Tiffany woke from her dream of yachting on the Amalfi Coast, being ravished by a dark, brooding sort who looked suspiciously like Rowdy, she'd find herself being assaulted by Mr. Bojangles's overexcited tongue.

"Sorry," Rowdy said. "I tried getting him off of you, but it was tough while trying not to spill your tea."

"I understand." After setting her dog on the pillow beside her, she struggled to push herself up in the bed. "Thank you. You didn't have to go to so much trouble."

He shrugged. "Pearl did all of the work. I just carried it upstairs." After placing her still-steaming tea on the nightstand, he asked, "Cookie or muffin?"

"Both." She frowned. "I'm horrible. Once this baby pops out, the carb police are going to lock me in solitary confinement for a year with nothing but celery."

"Knock it off. You're beautiful." After delivering her baked goods, he sat on the ultra-feminine chaise where Gigi usually lounged. At first he looked uncertain about what to do with his long legs, but then he figured it out and leisurely stretched as if he'd taken lessons on being a royal from her spoiled-rotten dog.

He cast her an indecipherable grin.

"What's that about?"

"What?"

"That grin. You look suspicious."

He crossed his legs. "You're way off base."

"Okay, then, what's up?"

"I'm not touching that with a ten-foot pole—especially when you're currently giving me a rather lengthy one." He winked.

It took her a sec, but then she flung a pillow at him. "You're horrible! How can you think of sex when I'm huge?"

"Because you're still the hottest woman I've ever seen, and when I walked in the room, your expression reminded me of the morning I woke up beside you—not to mention the crazy shit we did the night before."

Her cheeks flamed. Not that she protested him finding her ginormous body desirable, but she had to add, "In light of what we just went through with Susie and Jeb and my football-sized feet, how is any of that relevant?"

"How is it not?" He sat up, swinging his legs around to plant his feet flat on the floor and elbows on his knees. "Think about it. If it wasn't for that night, the two of us might never have spoken again. That has to mean something, don't you think?"

"Like in a touchy-feely universal kind of way?"

"Exactly. What if we're soul mates? And our son is the thread binding us together?"

"Soul mates?" She struggled not to laugh. "My future soul mate is waiting for me back in Texas. He will own a twenty-room Dallas mansion, a log cabin in Aspen and a French château we don't visit as often as we'd like, because it's so fabulous that it's always being rented for movies."

He rolled his eyes. "I refuse to believe you're that narrow-minded when it comes to finding a good man."

She didn't used to be. Back when Crawford asked her to marry him, she'd still believed in happy endings. "Right about the time Big Daddy landed himself in jail and Crawford served divorce papers, I gave up on love. It's an antiquated emotion best saved for sappy greeting cards. I'll be the first to admit, the night you and I shared was incredible—hands down, best sex I've ever had. But what did that get me? A bun in the oven and some navy SEAL cowboy who won't stick around any longer than the horse-riding version. If I told you this second I want to keep our baby and ride off into the sunset with you, what would you say?"

"Depends. Would this marriage have benefits?"

"No." She frowned. "Give me your real answer. Not the first one that pops into your dirty mind. Or your heroic, save-the-world SEAL mind. Take both of those what-you-think-you-should-do urges out of the equation to give this topic rational thought. What happens when our little Johnny has a bad flu or lands the lead role in his school play or is—"

"Since this is my son we're talking about, he'll be a quarterback like his old man."

Now she was rolling her eyes. "You didn't let me get to the heart of the matter. Let's say I did believe in love and marriage. With you gone the vast majority of the time, what good does a piece of paper do me when I need a hand to hold when Johnny's got the ball, there's five seconds left on the clock and his team is down by two points? If he makes the game-winning touchdown, who do we party with? If he doesn't and his whole team blames him for the loss, who do I console him with? Oh, sure, you're more than willing to step up and do the supposed right thing by marrying me—giving our baby your name and a roof over his head—but have you ever stopped to think about what that even means? I've been brutally honest with you about the fact that I'm not sure I have what it takes to be a parent—let alone a single parent. If I married you, wouldn't I essentially be signing up for just that?"

ROWDY DIDN'T HAVE an answer for her, so he mumbled an awkward goodbye, kissed her cheek, then fed her some BS line about needing to meet his brother to get his truck from her office lot.

The second he'd slipped from the house without being caught by Gigi or Pearl, he did call his brother for a ride, but he started walking in the hopes of clearing his mind.

He didn't want to admit it, but Tiffany's speech made a lot of sense. With him constantly deployed, she would be a single parent. But hell, he knew lots of guys who were married and had kids and they seemed happy enough. Grady and Jessie. Wiley and Macy. But Grady had chosen to leave the navy and Wiley had been forced out by an injury.

Rowdy didn't just love his job as a SEAL but needed it.

The rush.

It was the closest thing to being Rambo that America had to offer. The United States government gifted him the latest weaponry and cutting-edge gadgets. He worked with a band of brothers who would literally give their lives for him in a crisis. Hazard pay was pretty damned sweet, too. What else did Tiffany think made him able to afford the cozy house he planned to buy?

The thought of going without all of the above—quitting cold turkey—made him nauseous. What would he do with himself all day? How would he handle what most people considered a normal life when to him, *normal* meant disarming a terrorist nuke with ten seconds to spare?

He'd stormed his way past the neighborhood and now walked alongside the highway leading out of town. Tall weeds made the hike a struggle, but he was used to a lot worse.

A truck towing a horse trailer whizzed by. The resulting breeze was damned cold, so he jammed his frozen fingers in his jeans pockets.

His most pressing hardship wasn't the rapidly falling temperature but the turmoil in his mind. In figuring out how to keep his son while still hanging on to the career he held dear. And what happened with Tiffany? Beyond their chemistry between the sheets, what would make a marriage between them work? And he was talking a real marriage—like what his folks shared. Carl and Justine. But in order to get that kind of lasting relationship, what was he prepared to give? What, beyond his paycheck, was he willing to leave on their familial table?

A couple miles farther, he winced as Carl approached and the old farm truck's lights blinded him. "Little brother, you are one crazy SOB."

"Tell me about it." Rowdy held his hands in front of blasting heater vents.

"What'd your gal do this time that got you all wound up?"

How did he answer without making himself look like an ass? Hell, maybe he was an ass? "We were right in the middle of what's starting to be our usual debate when she tells me she's never wanted to be a single mother. No shit, right? I wouldn't especially want to be a single father. But if that's the case, then why shouldn't I be on board for giving our baby to this Jeb and Susie couple who seem a helluva lot better equipped to handle raising a child than either me or Tiffany."

Carl gunned the vehicle toward town. "I don't get this. When I picked you up from the airport, you were all about keeping your son. Now you're filled with doubts?"

"I can't help it. Tiffany does raise valid points. Plus, how do I stay in the navy while having a kid?"

"Did you honestly just ask such an asinine question? I'm not saying it would be easy, but thousands of active military and veterans manage just fine. So if that's your biggest parenting hurdle? I'm not buying it. Did you ever think it's time to man up and claim your son?"

"Well, yeah. That's why I'm here. But what if Tiffany's right? And our son would be better off being raised by another couple? They've got time and money."

"If you ask me, you're both being selfish."

"Selfish? What the hell? If anything, we're being *selfless*."

"Whatever. I'm sick of hearing about it. If you were man enough to get Tiffany pregnant, then you should be man enough to put your son's needs ahead of your own."

They'd almost reached Tiffany's office.

Despite Thanksgiving being two weeks away, downtown merchants had already swapped Halloween decorations for Christmas. The rush toward the holidays made Rowdy all the more incensed. Why the hell was everything in his life set on fast-forward?

What was wrong with him that he equated the birth of his newborn son with a sort of death? If he wanted to be a dad, his days as a SEAL seemed destined to die. As for the fact that Rowdy struggled to decide which life path he most wanted, did that make Carl right? Was he selfish?

He and his brother had always had their minor squabbles, but this felt different.

Carl pulled his truck behind Rowdy's.

Without a word, Rowdy climbed out and slammed his door.

Carl shouted out the now-open passenger-side window, "Call Mom if you're going to be late. She worries!"

Having delivered his cargo and message, Carl gunned from the lot, leaving Rowdy eating his exhaust.

He should've at the very least flipped Carl a bird, but honestly? He was too drained to care. Count on his big brother to twist the guilt knife a little deeper as to his mother's worry.

One more nail in the coffin of his career?

He climbed into his vehicle and turned the engine. The starter clicked a few times before catching. Great. On top of everything else, he now had more truck problems?

Since his ride seemed to be running fine, Rowdy aimed for the ranch but changed his mind in favor of checking on Tiffany again.

After a quick call to his mother, he ended up at Pearl's.

Gigi opened the door. "Get in here, handsome. We wondered where you'd run off to."

"I had to get my truck." He hitched his thumb toward the street where he'd parked.

"Actually…" She grabbed his forearm, tugging him inside. The air smelled rich. Chicken and dumplings? His stomach growled. "I'm glad for this moment alone."

His formerly excited stomach fell. What was she up to?

"I've had to keep this under wraps, because Tiffany gets all bent out of shape when I use the color printer for nonessentials, but I think nothing could be more important than uniting the both of you with your child."

Beyond uncomfortable with the conversation, Rowdy cleared his throat. "Thanks. Can we talk later? Right now I've gotta check on Tiff."

"Leave her bedroom door open!" Pearl shouted from the kitchen. "No funny business until after the wedding!"

"Yes, ma'am." To hasten his exit, Rowdy took the stairs two at a time.

He entered Tiffany's domain to find her brushing Mr. Bojangles while softly humming.

He cleared his throat. "Hey."

"You're back."

He shrugged. "My brother, Carl, said a few things I wanted to run past you."

"Shoot." Her silly little dog looked ready to purr from pleasure. She set down his brush to grab a pint-size sweater from a basket on her nightstand, then fit it over the dog's head.

Moments earlier he'd known just what to say, but now he couldn't find the right words. Carl's accusation cut Rowdy deep. He couldn't be that direct with a pregnant woman who was already under too much stress.

"Well?" She'd finished dressing the dog and now held him to her cheek for a cuddle.

"You know how you keep telling me part of the reason you want to give our baby up for adoption is that you won't make a good mom?"

She bowed her head. "It's the truth."

"I call BS. You don't think what you do for your pet is mothering?"

"It's hardly the same and you know it." She set the pooch alongside her on the bed. "If I need to run an errand, I can take him with me or leave him with my mom or…"

"Exactly. You could also do the same with our son." He sat on the chaise, facing her. "Look, you've actually made surprisingly valid points with this whole adoption thing. So many that I'm seriously thinking about agreeing with your position. But then I get this gnawing ache…" He patted his chest. "I can't even conceive of my son—our son—being in this world without us. And then Carl said something…" Rowdy hadn't planned to repeat his brother's hurtful sentiments, but maybe she needed to hear them? Maybe she needed the same verbal punch? "He accused us of being selfish."

"What?" She sucked in her next breath fast enough to cough.

Mr. Bojangles barked.

"Are you kidding?" Her eyes shined with tears.

"Afraid not."

"The whole reason adoption is even on the table is because I realize maybe I'm not the best woman for the job. Isn't that being self-less?"

"Exactly." Rowdy finally exhaled. "That's what I said. I was pissed. Where does he come off getting in our business like that?" Too antsy to sit, he made the short trek to her dresser for a cookie, then took the tray to her. "Eat. You need to keep up your strength."

"Yes, sir." She took a cookie and muffin. "But as soon as this baby pops out, carbs are out of my picture."

"Whatever. But here's another thing. You

know I'm considering adoption as a viable option?"

She nodded.

"I want you to do the same in regard to keeping our son."

"Rowdy, we—"

"Trust me, I am one hundred percent on board with every shred of your rationale. No one's life stands to be changed more than mine by adding a wife and baby. But what if that change was positive? For both of us. We've given the whole adoption thing a good look, but it's only been a couple weeks since I've been back in your picture. What would it hurt for you to give my way a chance? Especially since for now, it would only be in your head."

A WEEK LATER, Tiffany still couldn't stop thinking about Rowdy's haunted expression.

She sat across from him in her obstetrician's

crowded waiting room. He made faces at a six-month-old in a carrier at his feet.

The little girl giggled every time he raised his eyebrows and stuck out his tongue.

That pang in his chest he'd talked about? She felt it now.

Would he be this playful with their son?

Her imagination went straight to a cozy shared breakfast with her making pancakes and him feeding the baby oatmeal. He'd make adorable vrooming truck noises for their son and little Johnny would giggle and kick in his high chair, squealing with delight. She'd deliver Rowdy's pancakes, and he'd wrap his arm around her waist, reeling her in for a thank-you kiss.

She closed her eyes and knew much too well the feel of his lips crushing hers in every variation. Dizzying pressure to a butterfly-soft whisper. His kisses made her lose her mind, and she'd all too willingly signed up for the trip. His lightest touch—

"Miss Lawson? The doctor's ready for you."

Jolted from her daydream, Tiffany touched her heated cheeks, then the baby.

"Want me to go with?" Rowdy asked.

"No." *Yes!* How adorable would it be watching him see their son and hear his heartbeat for the first time?

"What if I want to?"

"Suit yourself."

He waved goodbye to his adorable friend.

She waved back.

A knot lurked at the back of Tiffany's throat.

If they were to marry and set up a home and Rowdy left to go off to war, how hard would it be watching their son wave goodbye? She blinked back tears.

"You okay?" Rowdy asked. He'd placed his big hand in the small of her back. The simple gesture made her huge pregnant body feel small and protected.

"I'm good," she said, even though she clearly needed time away from the stupid-handsome man to clear her head and return her last shred of sanity.

It didn't escape her notice when he politely turned away during her weigh-in. He also knelt to help her slip off the ugly loafers she'd been reduced to wearing since they were the only shoes in her closet that fit.

In the exam room, after the nurse took her blood pressure and delivered the reading, he asked, "Is that normal?"

"Yep. Our momma is doing great." She handed Tiffany a floral hospital-style gown and heated blanket. "You know the drill. It shouldn't be too long until the doctor's in."

"Great. Thanks."

Tiffany glanced at the gown, then to Rowdy. "Mind stepping out?"

"It's not like I haven't seen it before," he said with a grin. "Just kidding. But in case you need help, I'll be right outside."

"Thanks." She changed as quickly as she could, given her condition. Her hot-pink socks that had seemed like a good match for the Baby On Board sweater, which had been the only clean one that still fit, now looked silly with her pale green gown.

She was attempting to heft herself back onto the exam table when Rowdy knocked, then poked his head back in the room. "All clear?"

"Sort of." She hugged the still-warm blanket, hating herself for wishing it were him. "Don't look at my butt."

"Wouldn't dream of it—though, for the record, it's an awfully cute butt."

"Rowdy!" she scolded in a loud whisper. "You can't say things like that."

"Why not?"

She didn't have an answer.

Luckily, the doctor knocked, then entered. "The nurse said your blood pressure is good. How are those poor feet?"

"Better. So can I go back to work?"

"Sure. But try keeping it to only a few hours a day. You're a Realtor, right?"

"Yes."

"We have a new physician joining our clinic. She's temporarily staying with family, but would you be able to show her something on Thursday?"

"I'd love to. Thank you. I'll get you a card when we're done so you can give your friend my contact information."

"Perfect." To Rowdy, the doctor said, "I haven't seen you around here before."

"I'm the baby's father."

"This is an interesting development." She helped Tiffany lie back on the exam table. "It's always more fun for Mommy when the daddy's around. Tiffany, I have to ask, have you changed your mind about the adoption?"

"I'm not sure," Tiffany admitted.

The doctor strategically placed blankets so as to reveal only the baby bump.

The nurse stepped in and quickly shut the door.

Usually, the exam room felt plenty big. The pale lilac walls were soothing, as were the dim lights and collection of four-leaf-clover photographs artfully grouped on the far wall.

Rowdy's presence overwhelmed her not only physically but emotionally. For some unfathomable reason, what she could describe only as giddiness rose from deep within her soul when the doctor rubbed ultrasound gel on her tummy, then waved the magic wand for Rowdy to get his first glimpse and listen of their son.

How would he react? Would he be excited? Nervous? A little scared?

"There he is…" the doctor said. The gallop

of her baby's little heart never failed to give Tiffany a thrill. Knowing she had to give him away, she'd purposely tried to disconnect, but with each visit, that task grew harder. "Well, Rowdy? What do you think?"

Thanks, Doc, for asking what my heart needs to know...

Chapter Ten

Rowdy tried not to crowd Tiffany's personal space, but when the doctor waved the ultrasound wand across her tummy and he not only saw his son but heard his heartbeat, Rowdy was a goner.

Tears stinging his eyes, he leaned closer.

The doctor had asked him a direct question, but he'd be damned if he could remember what she'd said.

"Speechless is always a fun response," she said with a laugh.

"I'm sorry, what?" Rowdy asked. "I'm kind of…" He wasn't sure what he was feeling. Mostly overwhelming happiness and then sadness for the uncertainty still in the air.

He looked to Tiffany. Her blue eyes shone with unshed tears and she'd drawn her lower lip into her mouth for a sexy nibble. God, she was a beauty.

"I'm not entirely sure if I'm seeing our kid's elbow or a hockey stick, but regardless, Tiff, you made a good-looking baby." He skimmed his hand atop the crown of her head. "Seriously, he's…" He could hardly speak past the well of emotions threatening to overflow. "He's great."

"Thanks." Tiffany beamed.

The nurse handed them each a tissue when neither did a good job of holding back silent tears.

"You two stop, or you're going to get me going," the doctor said. "Your baby's heart rate is strong and right where we need it to be. Everything else looks good. Rowdy, if I could get you to step out of the room, I need to take my exam down below."

It took him a sec to catch on. But then he bent forward to kiss Tiffany's forehead before leaving the room, secretly glad for the chance to regain his composure.

He raked his hands through his hair.

This was a game changer.

After actually getting a look at his son, he couldn't even think of handing him over after his birth. But was he ready for a lifelong commitment?

He paced the hall, wishing for an easy answer, but there was none.

His stomach lurched when the door opened and the doctor and nurse stepped out.

The nurse said, "Tiffany's good to go as soon as she's dressed."

"Cool. Thanks." Rowdy struggled to find his

next breath. Maybe he shouldn't have tagged along? Maybe he'd OD'd on the recommended dose of touchy-feely emotions for one day?

"Nice meeting you," the doctor said. "Hopefully, you plan on staying in town?" Her tone implied what her words hadn't directly asked. Was he going to play an active role in his son's life?

Yes.

I mean, probably.

What am I thinking? Absolutely.

But how? How did he dive right into a second marriage with a woman he hardly knew? How did he know he'd even like being a dad? But who was he to assume he had a choice? If he'd been man enough to share in making the child, then he had the moral obligation to raise him.

"Yeah," he mumbled. "It was good meeting you, too."

With the doctor and nurse gone, Rowdy was

back on his own and brushing his sweating palms against the thighs of his jeans. His pulse galloped as fast as his son's and his mouth had gone dry.

He was a navy SEAL—supposedly one of the toughest men on the planet. So why did this issue have him feeling weak in the knees? His father and brother were much better equipped to handle this situation. But why? Especially when Rowdy had been trained to tackle any possible contingency with zero complaints. When he was assigned a mission, he'd never been the kind of guy to hem and haw. He was a soldier. He made a decision and saw it through. Period.

"Ready?"

"Yeah." He glanced up to find Tiffany leaving the exam room. Her long blond hair was tousled and her giant pink sweater hung crooked. Despite all of that, he'd never seen her look more beautiful. She was the mother of his child.

The freaking mother of his child.

She carried his precious son inside her body.

He took a moment to let that sink in. Was there any deeper intimacy a man and woman could share?

"Can you believe that just happened?" she asked.

"I know, right? Seeing our baby was—*wow.*"

"I try not to look. It's too hard, knowing I have to get off at the end of the ride."

"But you don't. We don't." They'd reached the end of the corridor and stood in a quiet corner leading to the patient checkout. "How can you tell me what happened in there didn't matter?"

"Of course it *mattered*, but to what end? Just because it's a modern-day miracle being able to see our unborn child doesn't change anything. It doesn't pay off Grammy's new mortgage or medical bills or—"

"Shh." He pressed the tip of his index finger over her lips.

She opened her mouth and nipped him. "Don't shush me. Especially when you know I'm right."

"What if you sell this new doctor a big, fancy house?"

"Realistically, what are the odds of her buying from me?" She tugged the front of her sweater. "*Webster's* has a picture of me under their definition of *hot mess*."

"Your defeatist attitude is getting old. I understand you're going through a rough patch, but you seriously need to work on your mental toughness."

"You need to stick your mental toughness where the sun doesn't—"

"Excuse me?" From behind them, a woman

cleared her throat. She pushed a stroller carrying twin infant girls.

Rowdy opened the door for her, then propelled Tiffany in the same direction. This constant bickering had to stop. It wasn't good for her or their baby.

When it was their turn at the checkout counter, the clerk asked, "Ms. Lawson, the doctor wants to see you again next week. What's a good day for you?"

Tiffany scheduled her appointment.

"What's going on with her bill?" Rowdy asked.

"It's been paid in full. We offer complete delivery packages." The number she read produced instant indigestion that made him feel as if his son were a box on a shelf. Right here and now, he'd send the message that his child was no longer for sale.

"I need to call my bank out east and transfer

funds, but is there any way to refund that previous payment and allow me to pay instead?"

"Rowdy, what are you doing?" Tiffany sported a Texas-sized scowl.

"I suppose we could," the clerk said. "But it's highly unusual. Let me check with my supervisor."

"Thanks," Tiffany said, "but there's no need for that. He's just messing around."

"No, Tiff, I'm not. I'm damned sick and tired of—"

"Sir…" The clerk raised her eyebrows, then nodded toward the waiting room's staring audience—many of whom were a G-rated crowd.

"Right. Sorry. I'll come back another time."

"What was that about?" Tiffany asked after reaching the privacy of his truck.

Much to her ever-increasing displeasure, Rowdy not only opened her door but scooped her up to set her on the tall vehicle's seat. She was still tingling from his touch when, once he sat behind the wheel, he further complicated matters by reaching over her to fasten her seat belt, in the process brushing his arms against her baby bump and breasts.

Nipples standing at attention, she crossed her arms.

The man made her all kinds of crazy.

When he turned the key in the ignition, it made a few clicking noises, which seemed to get him all riled up. Fortunately, on his next try, the engine turned over.

He drove them out of the clinic's crowded lot and through the few blocks leading to her grandmother's house, only to then turn onto the highway leading out of town.

"First," she said, "where are you taking me? And second, explain that stunt back at the obstetrician's."

"Where I'm taking you is a surprise that will hopefully, for once, shut you the hell up. And my *stunt* was the first step in reclaiming our lives. Jeb and Susie Parker might have put a down payment on our son, but effective today, he's off the market."

"I'm so sick of this." Pressing the heels of her hands to her throbbing forehead, she said, "One sonogram doesn't change a thing. Jeb and Susie have merely paid my medical bills because I couldn't. As for you implying I'm somehow profiting on the birth of our child?" She couldn't even look at his stupid face. And yes, she was purposely leaving out her usual *handsome* assessment, because after his latest streak of bad behavior, she no longer found him the least bit desirable.

Liar!

"I never said that, and you know it. Look at me."

"No."

"Tiff…" With far too tender a touch for her to keep a nice tight hold to her rage, he placed his hand under her chin, urging her to at least glance his way. "You put words in my mouth I would never say. I know the adoption is your way of doing what you wholeheartedly believe is best for our child. I know all these months without me, you have to have been worried out of your mind. But now I'm here. And I'm going to help. And you know what?"

She shook her head, swatting away his warm, gentle, stupid touch.

"For the rest of the day, you and I are going to stop fighting and work on becoming friends."

"Impossible."

"Try."

"I need to get home. Mr. Bojangles has started wriggling out of his sweaters and by this afternoon we're supposed to get more snow. I don't want him catching a chill." To calm the mental chaos the man never failed to produce, she nibbled her pinkie.

He shocked her by taking her hand, then slowly, with what to her chaotic pulse felt downright erotic, eased his fingers between hers. The heat, the electric awareness, the instant need, robbed her of all rational thought. When he further muddled her mind by raising her hand to his lips—those lips she knew all too well?

She closed her eyes and gulped.

I am Tiffany Lawson, she reminded herself.

I am a society darling.

I am strong and smart and talented and capable of caring for myself and everyone I love. I am fully in control of everything I do and say.

I don't want this man to hold me or kiss me or...

The second his lips touched the sensitive skin on the back of her hand, freeze-framed images of their wild night hit like a sensual firestorm.

For an instant, she squeezed her eyes shut.

Like my tongue here? Lower?

Turn around. I need to kiss you.

What if I brushed my lips across—

"Tiff?" he asked with a concerned glance her way. "You feeling all right? You look hot and splotchy."

"I'm fine." She snatched her hand free. "You focus on driving, and I'll worry about me."

"Yes, ma'am." His cocky sideways grin wrought all manner of havoc. She couldn't remember the last time she'd felt good old-fashioned desire, but an unforgettable humming between her legs reminded her of Rowdy's bedroom potential. "Why don't you take a nap? Bismarck's a fair piece down the road, and—"

"Why are we going there? I have to get ready for when my new client calls."

"That's exactly what we're going to do. Relax. Promise, you'll enjoy every second of the rest of our day…"

No truer words had ever been spoken.

An hour later, Rowdy had delivered her to a mall nail salon, where she was indulging in a decadent foot massage to be followed by a pedicure and manicure.

He sat patiently in the waiting area, flipping through fashion magazines as if he were actually interested. Every so often, he looked her way. When their gazes met, her body turned all hot and bothered. Thank goodness he was across the room, because she wouldn't know what to say. Had any man ever done something so thoughtful? No.

In Rowdy some lucky lady would land a real keeper. Too bad that woman wouldn't be her.

Why not? her buttinsky conscience nudged.

How many times had he asked to marry her? Offered to take care of her and their son? Marrying him would be easy.

Until it wasn't.

Until she went and did something reckless with her wounded heart by falling for him harder than she feared she already had. If she allowed feelings for him to ever pass this current superficial-physical-attraction stage? She'd be a goner. Her father and ex had taught her all too well what happened when men she loved abandoned her.

She wouldn't put herself through that kind of pain again.

The woman doing her pedicure raised her feet from the bubbling footbath to wrap them both in hot towels.

The sensation was beyond bliss and deep into a realm of unicorns and rainbows and lots and lots of still-warm-from-the-oven cookies.

Tiffany glanced up to find Rowdy staring.

His green eyes punched through her every excuse to stay away. And then he blew such a faint kiss that she couldn't be sure she hadn't imagined it.

Not only did her pulse surge, but the baby kicked.

Protecting her wary heart, she dropped her

gaze, only to raise it back up. To find his stupid, sexy grin and lose herself all over again.

For the rest of their time at the nail salon, she didn't look at him. She couldn't. The results were far too dangerous. The fact that he'd returned her to her natural salon habitat clearly had her punch-drunk on nail-polish fumes!

She'd opted for a fast-drying shellac finish, so as soon as Rowdy paid for her services, they reentered the bustling mall, which was already decked out for Christmas.

Santa reigned over the North Pole, aka former food court. Along with soaring mall-sponsored trees festooned in silver, powder-blue and white glittering ornaments stood hundreds of smaller trees that had been decorated in themes by different organizations. They all helped raise money for charity when mallgoers paid a dollar to vote for their favorites.

She put a dollar in the collection pot for the Barbie-themed tree.

Rowdy opted for a beach-themed tree that had sand and shells bunched around the base in lieu of a traditional skirt.

"It's Beginning to Look a Lot Like Christmas" played over the sound system.

Everywhere she looked, frazzled parents chased hyper kids.

Would that be her and Rowdy one day? Those moms and dads didn't look especially happy. They looked exhausted.

"Feel better?" he asked.

"Much. Thank you." Assuming he'd meant in regard to her nails, she avoided the deeper subject of the adoption that always lurked just beneath the glassy surface of their conversational waters. If she—they—did go through with giving their baby to Susie and Jeb, would she regret it? Would every holiday for the rest of her life be spent wondering *what if*?

He shrugged. "No biggie."

"To me it was." She forced a smile. Professionally manicured nails were a luxury she hadn't been able to afford for quite some time, and she refused to spend a moment more on worry. "Ready to head home?"

"Not a chance, princess. Your party's only just begun. While you were getting your nails and toes pretty, the ladies around me helped me out with the location of a maternity store. We're going to find you a few fancy Realtor dresses, a new coat—and shoes. Sensible, but still nice enough to make you feel like the ice queen I first met all those months ago."

He'd delivered his assessment in a playful tone, but she had to ask, "Is that how you saw me? As a coldhearted bitch?"

"There you go again." He bumped her shoulder with his upper arm. "Putting words in my mouth. You were dressed all in white, right down to those sky-high heels. In that run-down old bar, you looked like an angel. Unobtainable. Ethereal. So far out of my reach that I shouldn't have wasted my breath even talking to you. But I did, and we did and..."

She remembered the play-by-play of what happened next, and damn if her body wasn't craving a repeat performance.

In the center of the crowded mall, they'd stopped.

Turned to each other.

Was he going to kiss her? Here? In front of God, hundreds of families and Santa?

Please... her body yearned.

Don't even think about it, her carefully structured defenses railed.

She licked suddenly parched lips. Had he always been so tall? Had his chest always been so broad? Had he always smelled of sun-warmed leather?

He leaned closer.

She leaned closer.

He tilted his head.

She tilted hers.

He inched closer and closer until his warm breath tickled her lips and her heart thundered like a runaway herd of reindeer. She wanted his kiss more than anything, but badly enough to risk lowering the gate on her heart?

"Shoes," she blurted.

"What about them?"

"If you're sure—I mean, if you were serious about gifting me with a new work outfit—we should start with shoes." *Because if I stand here looking at your stupid-handsome, whisker-stubbled face for one second longer, I'll break. And then I'll be kissing you. And that wouldn't be good for either of us!*

"Right. Shoes. Lead the way…" He looked as dazed as she felt. *Had* he been on the verge of kissing her? Before her first marriage and divorce and this mess with Big Daddy, she used to know when a man desired her. Attraction had been second nature. As simple as knowing when she needed a cool sip of champagne. Now? For all she knew, Rowdy might have been pondering whether to have a cheese-burger or spaghetti for dinner.

A long waddle from their current location landed them in comfy leather seats with an eager salesman grabbing three pairs of shoes in various sizes. Fortunately, when it came to finding gorgeous shoes, her instincts were still sharp, and she'd found low-heeled black leather boots, somewhat-sensible black leather pumps and black flats.

"I like the boots," Rowdy said, "but how are those other two going to work in the snow?"

She waved off his concern. "Snow is no big deal. I just need to watch the heel height."

"If you say so…"

The salesman returned, and if it weren't al-ready bad enough that her normally perfect size-six feet had exploded into size nine, her calves and ankles had grown so huge that the boots wouldn't zip.

"Try again," she asked the college-aged kid. "Maybe the zipper's stuck?"

"Nah. They're too tight. My manager will kill me if I break it."

She cringed with embarrassment.

The salesman moved on to the heels. "You'll probably want to trade your socks for these." He wagged a pair of those crumpled pantyhose feet that looked like dead hamsters. The old Tiffany would have brought her own knee-high stockings. But then, in her defense, she hadn't exactly known their destination.

In regard to fit, her feet told the same sad story with a different shoe.

The baby wasn't due until January. At her body's current rate of expansion, how was she supposed to remain presentable till then?

Rowdy said, "I think you'd look cute in those red sparkly ones." He pointed to a corner shelf filled with jewel-toned shoe heaven. Most were stilettos, but there were a few flats. The red ones in question? Darling, but a bit over the top for your average Tuesday in Maple Springs.

"I don't know…" Tiffany grumbled. "They probably won't even fit. And they're way too dressy for work."

"Bring them in a size ten," Rowdy said.

"A ten?" Tiffany's eyes stung. "I wear a six."

"Correction." He patted her huge baby bump. "You used to wear a six. But for now, let's just try a ten, okay? Besides, it's not like anyone except me will even know the size."

"I guess you have a point. But still, they'd be way too fancy for work."

"Since when is Tiffany Lawson, rodeo queen, afraid of being fancy?"

"You have another point…" She couldn't help but smile.

The salesman returned.

She nibbled her pinkie while waiting for him to take the sparkling creations from a white satin drawstring case. The new-shoe smell served as the best possible aphrodisiac.

"Let me…" Rowdy left his chair, holding out his hand for the shoe.

"Of course." The salesman handed it over.

Grinning, Rowdy said, "This moment has Prince Charming written all over it, don't you think?" Kneeling, he'd clasped her foot, but not in a clinical trying-on-shoes way. More like a territorial stroking-her-sole-with-his-thumb kind of way, making her dangerously close to having a drag-him-into-the-nearest-janitor's-closet-for-a-make-out-session impulse. He finally slid on the left shoe and it must have been an early Christmas miracle, because it fit. "How's that feel?"

"Good." *Ridiculously good.* But she wasn't just talking about the shoe's cozy fit. She had to hand it to him, the man was skilled with his hands. "Put on the other."

He did.

Had it been possible for feet to sing, hers would have.

The power of her mani-pedi and new shoes was an intoxicating thing. In that moment, she remembered what it was like to have fun. She remembered how to laugh. Most important, remembered how good it felt to share her laughter with Rowdy.

"Well?" he prompted. "The whole time I've known you, you've never been this quiet."

"I love them." She leaned forward, wrapping her arms around his neck for a hug. *I love you*, her heart sang. But she didn't. Not really. She was clearly still high from nail-polish fumes. Toss in new-shoe leather and that special something that was all Rowdy and she was lost. Rendered incapable of snark. Head bowed, she said, "Seriously, I know this must sound silly, but something about new shoes makes everything better. It wouldn't surprise me if we left the mall to find the sun shining and birds chirping in a balmy eighty degrees."

He laughed. "If that's true, I think the state would issue a new tax to keep your new-shoe fund afloat. Hell, you might single-handedly transform North Dakota into the next Florida." His words might be teasing, but the sultry heat stemming from his secure hold couldn't be more real.

She backed away before her body grew any more at home in his arms.

The salesman returned. "How did they work?"

"Like a charm," Rowdy said. "Let's take two more pairs. Black and that funky green."

"Rowdy, no. That's too much."

"Welcome to life with me, darlin'. My wicked plan is to spoil you rotten."

As much as Tiffany liked the sound of that, she couldn't let down her guard. She couldn't trust that Rowdy's charm didn't come with a price far higher than shoes. It was no secret he didn't want to go through with the adoption. She had to make him understand that neither did she—not really. Not in the deep-down, quiet moments of her heart. But she was backed into a corner and nothing about her once carefully structured adoption plan now felt right. The only thing currently making sense was profusely thanking Rowdy, then accepting his proffered hand.

With the shoes purchased and bagged, strolling through the bustling mall with her naked palm pressed to his made it easy to envision him always being in her life. She could far too easily picture them this time next year, when they'd try holding hands but it would be too awkward while pushing a stroller and gathering up their dozens of Christmas packages. She'd have a thriving real estate business and he'd— That's where the dream died.

What would Rowdy do for work if he gave

up his job as a SEAL? Would he join his father and brother on their family ranch? Would he use the money he'd saved to start his own cattle ranch?

Bing Crosby crooned "Silent Night" over the mall's sound system. The song, the nagging questions, sobered her mood.

If Rowdy did take an early retirement from the navy, how long would it be until dissatisfaction with his new line of work turned to resentment for her and their son? After that, it would be only a hop, skip and jump to their inevitable divorce.

Tiffany had to face facts. No matter how delectable this very moment might be, once she surrendered her heart, all roads eventually led to her emotional ruin.

"Why so glum?" he asked. "Don't tell me your new-shoe glow already wore off?"

She forced a smile. "Not at all. I was actually thinking about how nice this is. Being with you. Taking in all the decorations." Hormonal tears wet her cheeks.

"Hey…" He dropped her hand so he could dry them with his thumbs. The shoe bag dangling from his wrist bumped the baby, causing them both to grin. "If we're having such a nice time, what's with the waterworks?"

I'm afraid you're going to leave me.

Even worse, she was terrified it wasn't her he wanted but their baby. Like some girls wanted to get married only for their fancy wedding, maybe holiday cheer had him enamored with the Norman Rockwell ideal of having a family?

"Tiff?"

"I'm good." She sniffed. "Let's get something to eat. My treat—meaning, corn dogs."

He laughed. "No offense, but there's a surprisingly good steak place just past the next fountain. Then we need to find new duds to go with your shoes."

"You've already done too much."

"Baby…" There they were, once again standing face-to-face in the throng. Her heart beat at an alarming rate. Only this time, her galloping pulse had little to do with their son and everything to do with the baby's father. She instinctively leaned closer, raising her chin.

Are you ever going to kiss me?

Chapter Eleven

Damn.

Through what had felt like an endless meal, Rowdy struggled to focus on his steak rather than Tiffany's mouth. Her perfect mouth, with full, kissable lips…

Candlelight wasn't helping his frustration.

Neither was the dark paneling or wandering classical guitarist.

All of it set a mood that was essentially a lie.

A glance in Tiffany's direction showed her to be oblivious to the restaurant's romantic vibe.

She happily munched her steak, chatting about whether slacks or a dress would look best with her shoes.

"I'm thinking slacks. A nice flat is always a cute pairing, don't you think?"

"Huh?"

"Haven't you heard a word I've said?"

"Sure." He'd heard lots of words. He just didn't much care about any of them. "Are you going to eat your bread?"

"No. Go for it."

He did. And when she changed the topic to the option of blouses or sweaters, he'd had just about all any reasonable man could take of discussing fashion.

"You ever think about it?" he blurted.

"What?"

"The night we…" he pointed toward the baby "…you know."

"Oh…" Her cheeks reddened. "Well, sure, but I try not to. It was a mistake. All of it. I never should have gone to that bar, and I sure shouldn't have gotten that motel room with you."

"Why not? Are you saying it wasn't a good time?"

She refused to meet his gaze.

"I'll take your silence as an admission that you enjoyed it as much as I did but you're too stubborn to admit it."

She shook an obscene amount of steak sauce onto her meat.

"In fact, if we were to end up back in a motel room, alone, with nothing better to do than take advantage of each other, I'll bet you'd do it all over again."

"Never."

"Wanna bet?"

"No—but only because I don't have the cash to blow on something so frivolous."

"Then you're admitting you'd lose?"

"Not at all. I'm just saying it's a dumb bet."

He eased back in his chair and smiled. "You'd be all over me, and you know it."

She sighed. "If you're done, can we please get back to shopping? The mall's probably closing at nine and it's already seven."

"Yes, ma'am." He signaled the waiter for the check, then took the last few bites of his meat.

Ten minutes later, they were back to fighting holiday shoppers. "Jingle Bells" blared over the sound system and no fewer than six kids were pitching screaming fits over wanting to see Santa.

He found a map of the mall's layout and located the only maternity store.

When they finally made their way there, the long walk was worth it, judging by the size of Tiffany's smile.

"Just look at all of this. I found my other maternity stuff at thrift stores, but the sizes were always off. How exciting is it to get to try on something new?"

"Sorry," he said while she sorted through a rack of holiday-themed sequined sweaters.

"About what? You're beyond sweet for bringing me here. Really, I can't thank you enough."

"I wish I had been here with you from the start—sharing everything. Your first doctor visits and buying maternity clothes and baby gear. Painting his nursery and assembling his crib."

"But why would you have done all of that when he's not even ours?"

"He'll always be ours, which is another reason why this whole adoption thing is unnerving. I can't wrap my head around how it would feel this time next year without him."

"What about me?" She covered her mouth. "I didn't mean to say that out loud."

"It's a legitimate question. And for the record—yes, I would miss you. You're argumentative, sassy, sometimes don't make any sense and infuriatingly stubborn. Despite all of that, Tiffany Lawson, you're growing on me."

"Aw, thanks." She elbowed him. "You had me at new shoes."

From where she summoned the energy to try on so many clothes, Rowdy would never know, but by the time they left the store, she'd found a coat and two outfits to match each pair of shoes. Most of it had been on sale, even though he'd told her he didn't care about the price. In his experience, a lot of women would have taken him for all they could. He liked her even more for the fact that she didn't try to take advantage of him.

"Hope you remember where we came in?" she said as they paused to get their bearings alongside a giant candy cane.

"We need to take a left by Santa's workshop."

"That's right. I remember thinking how much I'd like a candy cane."

"Want me to get you one?"

"Would you?"

He handed an "elf" a five-dollar bill for a handful. "Think this will be enough?"

"You're amazing. How can I ever thank you?"

I can think of a few ways.

"I mean, back when I had all the money in the world, I took shopping for granted. Now I realize what a big deal it is to look and feel my best, and…" Her eyes shone with tears. "Thank you."

"You're welcome." He tried wrapping her in a hug, but it was tough with not only the baby but shopping bags between them. "You're going to sell this new doctor a big house, and the commission will keep you afloat for months."

"From your lips to God's ears."

They continued the hike to the car only to round the last corner and freeze.

"Is that what I think it is?" Rowdy asked.

"I knew snow was in the forecast, but the

weatherman said nothing about a *snowpoca-lypse*."

Apparently, the entire time they'd been in the mall, Mother Nature had dumped white stuff. They'd already gotten a good two feet, and more thick flakes fell by the minute.

"Wait here." He parked Tiffany on a bench in the heated vestibule, then set the packages beside her. "I'm going to get the truck. Don't leave this spot until you see me pull up outside, okay?"

She nodded.

Not wanting to haul his coat around the mall, he'd left it in the truck. Now Rowdy sorely missed it. Frigid air mixed with high winds meant his teeth were chattering only halfway to his destination. Holy hell, it was cold. He'd need to get the truck nice and toasty before bringing Tiffany outside.

Plows worked the lot, but with so many cars it was a losing battle. They'd piled snow behind the smaller vehicles and now dozens were stuck.

He reached his pickup and climbed behind the wheel to ram the key into the ignition, but instead of a satisfying roar, all he got was clicking.

Great. His wonky starter was now officially busted.

Over an hour from home.

In the middle of a blizzard.

He slammed the heel of his hand against the dash, then slipped on his coat before trudging back to the mall to deliver the news.

But when he reached the vestibule? The exact bench from where he'd specifically told her not to move? She'd moved.

Tiffany and all of her shopping bags were gone.

THE LINE FOR the bathroom was insane.

At least fifteen women and little girls deep.

The handles from her heavy bags were digging lines into her palms and her feet had started to swell.

By the time she finished, washed her hands, then started the long walk back to where Rowdy had left her, each step felt like a hundred.

Never had she been happier to see his scowling face approach. "Where the hell did you go? I told you not to move."

"You can't tell a pregnant lady's bladder not to move. I had to go—bad." Relief shimmered through her when he took the bags.

"Okay, well, you scared the hell out of me. I thought you'd been abducted."

"Right. Because so many stalkers have the hots for giant pregnant women." She waddled to a seating area and collapsed into an armchair.

"What's wrong? You look pale."

"I'm exhausted but otherwise all right. Did

you get the truck?" She couldn't wait to get home, have a nice long soak in Pearl's roomy claw-foot tub, then cuddle with Mr. Bojangles.

"About that…"

"You couldn't find it? Were you in the wrong lot?"

"Not exactly."

"Hurry up and tell me before I have to pee again."

He gave her the CliffsNotes version.

"Let me get this straight. Even though you knew the starter was going out, you thought it was a great idea to take your truck on a road trip?" She took her phone from the small purse she wore slung across her chest. "I could call Jeb and Susie. He has a four-wheel drive. I'm sure they'd be happy to help."

"I have no doubt they would, but I've got everything handled. There's a Holiday Inn across the street. I already made a reservation and called a towing company, but because of the snow, they're pretty backed up."

"Did you get two rooms? Because I'm not sleeping with you."

"Yes, as a matter of fact, you are. They only had one room available, and it has a king-size bed."

"Rowdy Jones, if this is all some elaborate ruse to—"

"Trust me, if I wanted in your pants that bad, I'd already be there." He winked.

"Pig."

"Oink, oink." He held out his hand to help her from the chair. "Come on. The hotel runs a mall shuttle every thirty minutes. I don't want to miss it."

She tried getting up from the deep chair without his assistance, but her efforts proved to be an epic fail.

He abandoned her shopping bags to plant his

hands under her arms, hefting her up and out. "Damn, our son's getting big."

"Thanks. Tell me something I don't know."

They bickered back to the vestibule. While he helped her into her new red coat. During the short ride to the hotel. While waiting in line to get registered. Again in the elevator and all the way down the long corridor leading to their room.

"Here we are…" He opened the door with a flourish. "Home, sweet home."

Even from the shadowy light rising from the brightly lit parking lot, she saw the room was a step up from the last one they'd shared.

He reached around her to flip on an overhead light switch for the hall leading from the bathroom to the bed and sitting area.

She veered to her left, allowing him to pass on her right, praying he wouldn't brush against her—not because it didn't feel good. But because it always managed to feel so right.

Her attraction for him felt wrong on a zillion different levels. It distracted her from what was most important—caring for her mother and grandmother. Keeping them safe. If her grandmother lost her home...

The mere thought was enough to cue hormonal tears.

She ducked into the restroom and closed the door.

"Tiff?" Rowdy's voice was muffled. "Everything okay?"

"Fine." Only it wasn't. Because she was trapped in a warm and cozy hotel room with a man who made her lose all rational thought. What she needed was to redirect her attention on to anything other than him. So she filled the tub with steaming water, squirting in the peach-scented body wash the hotel had provided.

Once she'd stripped and then sunk up to her neck in delicious-smelling bubbles, for an instant, the hot water made her wholly content. Then she realized her baby bump rose from the suds like an island. And then her mind skipped to the stupid-handsome man who'd helped make her baby.

"Tiff?"

"Yes?" Her cheeks blazed hotter than the water.

What had she been thinking? How was getting naked supposed to make her think of anything other than Rowdy?

"I called your grandmother to let her know you wouldn't be home until tomorrow."

"Thanks." She'd called on their way to the mall to let the two women in her life know she'd be late, but never had she intended to be gone overnight.

"I know it's only been a few hours since we ate, but I'm hungry and thought you might be, too? I ordered a pizza. Hope sausage and mushroom is all right?"

"Sure." Every inch of her glowed. The mere sound of his voice made her crave more of him.

Eyes closed, she gulped.

"Tiff?" His voice sounded clearer. Almost as if he were alongside her in the room.

Wait—he wouldn't dare. Would he?

Eyes wide open, she found him near the sink, holding his hands over his gaze.

"Go away!" she shrieked, covering her embarrassingly huge breasts with her hands.

"I wanna see the baby."

"Are you crazy?"

"Just one peek."

"No."

"Please?"

"Absolutely not."

"Just one little peek, and I promise to leave you alone."

"Rowdy…"

"Come on. No funny business. I just want to see my son."

"All you can see is my giant stomach. It's not all that attractive."

"Bull. I'll bet your body is even more beautiful now than it used to be." He'd come perilously close and now crouched a mere foot from the tub. His voice was smooth and decadent. Warm caramel. She pressed her legs closer in what she feared to be a futile effort to stop the needy hum. "Let me see, Tiff…"

"Okay, but…" *Please, don't hurt me by telling me how fat I've gotten or how my stretch marks turn you off or—*

He sharply exhaled. "Damn, you're sexy. Already a MILF."

"I'm not." *But I appreciate your fib.*

He'd repositioned onto his knees and pressed his big hand atop the baby. His every fingerprint strummed her with awareness. Pleasure. Cravings for more of anything he had to offer.

He kept his hand on the baby, but his fingers

drifted higher. Her nipples puckered beneath her palms.

"I want to kiss you."

Their gazes locked.

I want that, too.

"And then I want to carry you to the bed and figure out a position that allows me to bury myself inside you."

She licked suddenly parched lips.

"I promised Pearl we'd behave, but…" he played dirty by flashing his stupid-handsome grin "…you know what they say about promises."

They were made to be broken.

What would it hurt to be with him one more time? What was the worst that could happen? It wasn't as if she could get any more pregnant.

"Talk to me, Tiff. What are you thinking?" He slid his hand lower, to the V between her legs. Without saying a word, she answered his question by opening for him.

The instant he touched her, she lost all ability to think or speak. And when he leaned in to hover his lips above hers, she refused to care about anything other than finally getting his kiss.

At least until a knock sounded on the room's outer door.

A man called, "Pizza delivery!"

"Shit." He looked to the door, then her. "Don't budge. I'll be right back."

With him gone, her sanity returned along with her ability to breathe.

He'd closed the bathroom door, so she gripped the tub's safety bar to pull herself up, then as quickly as possible toweled herself dry. She was just attempting to draw up her panties when Rowdy rejoined her.

"I was afraid of this." He stepped disturbingly close and smelled of the strongest aphrodisiac on the planet—pizza. "As usual, you refuse to follow directions." He settled his big hands low on her hips and then drew her as close as the baby allowed.

With only her towel between them, her pulse went haywire. "Rowdy…" She licked her lips. "Maybe this isn't such a good idea? Being around you like this… I—I can't think."

"For once, what would it hurt for you to stop analyzing and simply *feel*?" His warm breath fanned her upper lip.

She ached from the effort of denying her attraction. She didn't just want to kiss him—she wanted to lose herself to him. She wanted to forget everything but how right they felt together—at least physically.

Everything else could sort itself out later.

Here, now, she pressed her palms to his chest, fisting his shirt when he inched still closer.

Anticipation for his kiss balled in her chest. *Kiss me*, her soul cried.

And then he did.

He slanted his lips atop hers, and in that instant, she'd found home. A butterfly-soft brush morphed into a fevered, desperate give-and-take as she helped Rowdy strip and then he made good on his earlier statement to carry her to bed.

They bumped and fumbled and kissed, only to find it wasn't all that easy for him to enter her in a conventional way. Finally, necessity provided a solution when he helped her straddle him, then settled in for a nice long ride.

With his hands on her hips, he plunged deeper.

She closed her eyes and tipped her head back, abandoning herself to the heady sensations that only he'd ever been able to give.

How heavenly would it be to wake to this kind of pleasure every morning and fall asleep the same way each night? Truly giving herself to him would be way too easy. It was his leaving that would be impossibly hard.

Just like every other man she'd loved, he would eventually leave…

Her climax struck with such exquisite beauty that tears stung her closed eyes.

He stiffened, tightening his hold before releasing a rugged sigh. "Damn. What you do to me is criminal."

"I'm sorry?" she said with a half laugh. "If it helps, you do the same to me."

He sat up a little, and she leaned down a little, touching her forehead to his.

"You do know I won the bet."

"What bet?"

"Remember the wager we made back at the mall? About how if we ever ended up back in a motel room, that we'd…" He winked.

"Hush. It was stupid. And I never agreed."

"Doesn't matter. I still won."

"Whatever."

He spiraled a few locks of her hair around

his pinkie. "Does this mean you changed your mind?" he asked.

"About what?"

"Marrying me. You know it's the right thing for the baby. Plus, we'd get to have great sex."

It's the right thing.

We'd get to have great sex.

Nowhere in his speech did he mention having fallen deeply, madly in love. Not that it would have mattered. She'd been told she was loved by lots of guys. It wasn't the words that mattered but actions.

"Tiff? Marry me?"

Swallowing hard, she shook her head. "Could you please help me to the restroom? I think I'm going to be sick."

Chapter Twelve

Rowdy was no saint.

He'd seen plenty of freaky things in his thirty-odd years. But having a woman puke her guts out right after they'd made love? That ranked right up there with slogging a fully-loaded raft across a lake bed that turned out to be more mud than lake.

"Babe, what can I get you?" he asked from his seat on the edge of the tub.

"Do something with my hair. I'm hot."

It was on the tip of his tongue to ask what

specifically she wanted done, but self-pres-
ervation told him this was one of those times
when he'd be better off figuring it out for himself.

When she sat back on her knees in front of
the commode, he readjusted the blanket around
her slim shoulders, then finger-combed her
long hair back, weaving it into a braid. His
friend Grady had a little girl who'd taught him
the skill.

"Thank you," she said. "I'm sorry."

"You're welcome and you've got nothing to
apologize for." He stood and wet a washcloth
with cold water. Stroking her forehead and
cheeks, he said, "Think it was something you
ate?"

"Probably. I gobbled twice my weight in butter."

"Then I guess I'm lucky you didn't melt?"

Her slit-eyed gaze only encouraged him.

"Get it? The two of us together were so hot that—"

"I get it." Silent tears shimmered on her cheeks.

"Hey..." Sobering, he set down the washcloth to sit beside her, drawing her into his arms. "If you're hurting that bad, need me to call for help?"

She shook her head. "I don't know why I'm crying. It's stupid. Hormones have turned me into a lunatic."

"If it helps—" he kissed her left temple "—when my brother's wife was pregnant, she nearly ran him out of the house. She was always hopping mad about something. He's got a thing for beef jerky, but if he so much as had it in the same room as her, he'd have hell to pay."

Tiffany laughed. "Smells are bad. They're all magnified. Like I'm a great big basset hound."

"You are cuddly." He gave her an extra-firm squeeze. "But I don't see any drool."

She gave his forearm a light swat. "Don't make me laugh."

"Yes, ma'am." He kissed the crown of her head. "Want me to run you another bath?"

"Yes, please. And when I'm feeling better, I promise to do something nice for you."

Like marrying me? Keeping our son?

What would it take for her to see both items needed to be on her agenda? Or was he jumping the gun? Had being with her again in the biblical sense made him think they'd created a bond that wasn't really there? Oh—make no mistake, he wanted it to be. But it wasn't the kind of thing a man could force.

He'd already been with one woman who hadn't been all that into him. Was he really up for reliving that scenario?

"ROWDY?"

"You're a royal pain in my ass," he said into his cell before wiping sweat from his brow with his flannel shirtsleeve. It had been four days since they'd talked. In that time, Tiffany had avoided his calls, dodged repeated visits to her family home and even driven the other way when she'd seen him walking down the street toward her office. "What's up with the evasion tactics?"

"I don't know what you mean."

"The hell you don't." He leaned on the end of his pitchfork. He'd once again landed the crap job of mucking out the barn stalls. It had only served as a reminder that if he stayed here in town, this was what he had to look forward to for the next fifty years. "Why did you even call?"

"I have news."

"Oh?" Had Jeb and Susie backed out of the adoption? If that was her news, part of him would be elated to keep his son. Another part of him? Well, that guy was still scared shitless by the prospect of becoming a father.

"Remember that new doctor who was coming to town? And how she needed a new house?"

"Did you sell her one?" The words spilled out of him in a rush.

"I think so. We have one more to see tomorrow, but she loved the one we saw today. It was amazing—a modern log cabin with great big windows and a river-stone foundation. First class all the way. It looked like a five-star ski lodge."

"Nice." *So why are you calling?*

"It really was. She has three kids. Her husband's a doctor, too."

And? Get to the point.

"Thanks again for the new shoes, coat and clothes. If I do end up with the sale, I'll have your generosity to thank."

"Any man in my position would have done the same." Or more. He'd barreled into town intent on making an honest woman of her and giving his son a proper last name. Now more times than not, he felt all messed up inside. Like the yard after a nasty storm. Filled with fallen twigs and debris. Cluttered and chaotic.

"Maybe. But you did. So, thanks."

After an uncomfortably long pause, he forced his lungs full of the chilly barn air. "Is that why you called? About the clothes?"

She blurted, "Remember how your brother called us selfish?"

"Yeah." Mad all over again, he tightened his grip on the fork's handle.

"Well, I was in the middle of a house tour, making polite small talk, when we entered this awesome home theater. It was seriously pimped out. Built-in leather recliners, curtains over the screen—even a popcorn machine and movie-butter dispenser."

"Sweet."

"She started talking about how much her kids would love the room, and then she got all misty-eyed, telling me how much she missed them. I asked how she did it—worked such a demanding job while raising three kids. She said her kids were her reason for living. And that sometimes it was hard juggling family and work responsibilities but that she and her husband wouldn't have it any other way. The rest of the afternoon, her words stayed with me. And I thought about how I have been avoiding you—not because I didn't want to talk to you and kiss you and do lots of other things we have no business doing, but because the God's honest truth is that I'm scared maybe your brother's right. Maybe we are selfish? Maybe if we really put our son's needs ahead of our own, nothing else would matter but him?"

Lips pressed tight, Rowdy tugged the brim of his battered leather cowboy hat.

"Aren't you going to say anything?"

"I like that you've at least been thinking about me."

"Rowdy, I'm serious. When my client went

on and on about how her kids matter more than anything, I felt a pang in my chest that's still there. What if we sign those adoption papers but regret it? How would we cope with the guilt and loss?"

"Wish I had an answer for you." He really did.

His call waiting beeped. A glance at the screen showed a number he didn't want to see. His commanding officer's.

"Babe," he said, "I'm sorry, but can I call you back? My boss is calling."

"Sure. But don't forget."

He answered his CO's call.

Then he had his brother drive him to Bismarck Municipal Airport.

And parachuted into Africa two days later.

TIFFANY POUTED WHEN Rowdy hadn't called back within thirty minutes. She got a little teary when it was time to feed Mr. Bojangles his supper and Rowdy called, but before they'd said more than hello, the service dropped.

When a week passed, she was pissed but assumed turnabout was fair play. He must be playing a tit-for-tat head game. She'd avoided him, so now it was her turn to feel the burn.

But when two weeks passed, she made her first big house sale, Thanksgiving came and went, and she still hadn't heard from him, worry took hold. Had he fallen ill? Been in a wreck? Should she ask Pearl for his mother's number?

"Fretting never solved any problem," Pearl said as she took a fresh batch of oatmeal cookies from the oven. They reminded Tiffany of the time Rowdy had brought her cookies in bed. And how he was always doing nice things for her but she was always so snippy. "Neither did pretending you don't give two figs about a man when you clearly do."

"What man?" Tiffany asked from the table,

where she sat peeling potatoes. The last thing she needed was for Pearl to get wind of the fact that as much as she'd struggled not to fall for Rowdy, she'd been stupid enough to do that very thing.

There was so much she wanted to say to him, but he was gone. Had her constant complaining driven him away?

"If you worry any louder, you'll wake your lazy, spoiled-rotten mutt."

"Who said I'm worrying?" As for her dog, he slept on his zebra-striped pillow in front of the heater vent, oblivious to anything other than his own comfort.

"We've both noticed," Gigi said upon entering the room. "You haven't been yourself since Rowdy's been gone. But he'll be back soon, you know."

"What do you mean?" She hugged her baby. "Do you know where he is?"

"Of course. Don't you?"

"Mom, are you kidding me?" Tiffany tossed the peeler into the metal bowl.

"I just assumed you knew." Gigi joined her at the table. "You get so prickly every time I bring up the wedding that I didn't want to further upset you by bringing up the fact that Rowdy got emergency orders to ship out. His mom told me she doesn't even know where he went or when he'll be back. She hates how secretive he has to be, but I guess that's part of his job."

He left without telling me?

Right at this very moment, he could be in some godforsaken country alone in a ditch or hurt or…

She refused to even think the last part. If he were to die without seeing his son—their son— Her breath caught at the back her throat.

Pushing her chair back from the table, Tiffany made a mad dash for the bathroom to be sick.

TWO WEEKS BEFORE CHRISTMAS, Rowdy stood in line with at least four dozen fellow SEALs, awaiting his turn to place his trident on top of Duck's casket.

The chain of events that had led him to this place and time still didn't seem real. He couldn't wrap his head around the fact that one minute Duck had been asking him for a stick of Juicy Fruit, and the next they'd heard the pop of enemy fire and taken cover.

By the time Rowdy realized Duck was no longer beside him, it was too late. His body armor had done no good against a shitstorm of bullets.

Their team's plans had been precise.

They'd each played an assigned role and there shouldn't have been a problem. But there was.

Faulty intel led their team into a trap. It was a damned miracle more of them hadn't died.

In the belly of the Chinook chopper, Rowdy and Logan had held Duck's hand till the end.

The guy had a wife and four kids—one of them a girl, barely a month old.

He looked up to see Ginny, Duck's wife, standing stoically, bravely, as if her entire life hadn't shattered. She held the baby in the crook of one arm and the hand of their smallest son. The two oldest boys flanked her.

Her dark sunglasses hid her eyes but couldn't mask the glint of sun on silent tears.

The Norfolk, Virginia, day was ridiculously pleasant.

Birds chirped and a hint of a breeze waved countless American flags. The air smelled of freshly mowed grass and Logan's annoying aftershave.

Rowdy missed Tiffany.

He'd lost track of how many times he'd started dialing her number but stopped himself short. Whatever emotions simmered between them had to stop. It had taken a front-row seat to seeing one of his best friends dying to make

Rowdy understand how real shit had gotten. Committing to being a father wasn't a game.

It killed Rowdy that he hadn't been able to save Duck. He'd played the scene over and over in his head. If only he'd been closer, faster, more agile.

It was finally his turn to press his pin into the top of Duck's casket. The sign of respect was a time-honored SEAL tradition, but Rowdy hardly felt worthy. Duck's family haunted him. The boys looked just like him—right down to the blue eyes, freckles, sandy-brown hair and cowlicks on the right side of their teary faces.

Rowdy pressed his palm to the casket's sun-warmed wood.

I'm sorry, man. It all happened too fast. There was nothing I could do.

The knot in his throat made it tough to breathe.

"Dude…" Logan placed his hand on Rowdy's shoulder. "Let him go."

Rowdy nodded.

Let him go.

Logan's words were unwittingly profound. Yes. He had to let him go. Only Rowdy wasn't just talking about Duck but his son.

THE NEXT DAY, Rowdy was finally back in Maple Springs.

Big surprise, it was snowing. Hard.

So hard that he had to lean forward behind the wheel of his pickup to see the reflective poles marking the road's edge.

His mom's car had been in the shop for the past few days, and she'd gotten a Christmas-carol CD stuck in his truck's player. If he heard one more line about a drummer boy or figgy pudding, he'd shoot the damned thing out.

He'd been in a foul mood since getting back.

Everything felt out of whack. He hadn't been sleeping and foods no longer tasted right. He was no good to himself or anyone else. Every time he closed his eyes, he saw Ginny and those four fatherless kids.

When Rowdy finally reached Pearl's street, snow fell so fast the wipers had a hard time keeping up.

In front of the old house, he killed the engine, grabbed his overnight bag, then dashed for the house.

On the porch, he stomped snow from his boots, then rang the bell.

"Good gracious," Pearl said upon opening the door. "Why am I always finding you playing out in the snow?"

"Couldn't tell you, ma'am. Is Tiffany here?"

"Of course. She's in the office. Take off your coat and boots. I'll go get her."

Tiffany's dog barked himself silly, trying to attack Rowdy's feet. The mutt wore a hot-pink rhinestone sweater with a fur collar. The ridiculous sight gave Rowdy his first faint smile in what felt like a damned long time.

Rowdy scooped him up.

A rub behind his ears was all it took for the little dog to quiet.

"I could slap you into the next county," Tiffany said, practically waddling down the hall in a too-tight T-shirt and sweatpants. Her baby bump was huge, but her cheeks looked hollowed. Dark circles were under her eyes. "Why didn't you call?" As if maybe wanting a hug, she stepped in close but then backed away, hugging herself. "I've literally been worried sick."

"Sorry. Honestly, I figured you'd be glad having me out of your hair."

"You're an ass."

"Probably."

"I mean it. How dare you leave the country without telling me? What's wrong with you? What kind of father leaves his child without even saying goodbye?"

"I tried calling, but my battery died."

"Likely story. Ranks right up there with you losing your phone down a well. I hate you!"

"Tiffany Anne!" Gigi floated into the entry. She wore a red-sequined muumuu and carried a string of Christmas lights. The house smelled of cinnamon and fresh-baked bread. "Is that any way to talk to your fiancé?"

"Stay out of this, Mom. Rowdy was just leaving." She snatched the dog from his arms.

"The hell I am. Have you seen how hard it's coming down?"

"I don't care where you go," Tiffany said near the stairs, "but you're not staying here."

"Rowdy." Gigi pressed her hand to his forearm. "You are welcome to stay as long as you like—just remember, no relations until after the wedding."

"Yes, ma'am."

When Gigi headed back to the living room, Rowdy chased Tiffany up the stairs. "For looking about ten months pregnant, you're fast."

"Shut up. I hate you."

"No, you don't." He hovered behind her, making sure she didn't fall.

"I seriously do. I've been sick for days. Why? Because you're too damned inconsiderate to give me a single call." At the top of the stairs, she paused to catch her breath.

Mr. Bojangles had fallen asleep in her arms.

Rowdy hefted both of them into his arms, carrying them to Tiffany's bed.

"Put me down," she said, launching a half-hearted fight. But by the time she'd really worked up a head of steam, he'd already settled her on the mattress.

"We need to talk." He took a seat on the chaise.

"The time for talking was back in November. Now I'd just as soon spit on you as look at you."

"Fair enough. I'm sorry. When I left…" He glanced at the ceiling, wishing for an eloquent way to explain the chaos in his heart. "I thought I was sure about a lot of things. I wanted to marry you and raise our baby boy, but—"

"Now you don't?" She gulped, rubbing her palms over the baby.

He leaned forward, cupping his hands over hers.

The fascination, the heat, was still there. He couldn't deny he wanted her just as bad now as he ever had. But as long as he was a SEAL, he had no right becoming a dad. He'd seen the pain of losing their father etched on the faces of Duck's boys and they haunted him. As did the thought of his baby girl never truly knowing her father. She wouldn't have anyone to take to daddy-daughter dances or to give her away at her wedding. It was tragic. Only one thing could have stopped it—if Duck had never married or had kids at all.

After forcing a breath, he said, "I think we should go ahead with the adoption."

"What?" She shook her head. Tears shone in her eyes. "After our night together and I found out you were in danger, I realized we should keep our baby boy. I don't know what I feel for you, but I do know it was awful having you gone. Let's resume your house hunt. Find you a nice little ranch where your only real danger would be falling off your horse."

"Here's the thing." A muscle ticked in his jaw. "I need the danger. The revenge. I know I must sound sick, but I'm afraid it might be the only thing keeping me alive. My friend Duck—" His voice cracked with emotion. "He died. When it happened, it didn't seem real. It was like a video game. I watched him going down—it was in slow motion, blood gushing from his side. I kept thinking, *This isn't real. It can't be real.* But it was. And he—he died. And I..."

"Hey…" Tiffany left the bed to sit beside him on the chaise, wrapping him in a sideways hug. "I'm sorry. Death hits everyone in different ways."

"I guess." He leaned forward, sliding his hands into his hair. "My only real takeaway is that if he can die, so can I. How stupid is it that before losing Duck, the fact never sank in?"

"You've never seen other soldiers pass?"

"Sure, I have. But this was different. Before, I knew them, but they weren't close friends. I didn't know they preferred yogurt and granola for breakfast and listened to Aerosmith on endless flights. I didn't know they had a wife and kids waiting for them to come home. Only Duck never will. And that *kills* me." He rubbed his chest. "Losing him hurts so bad, but I have to keep it together. For you. For our son."

"You don't have to do anything," she softly said, "except let me take care of you. I've got this." As she cupped her hand to his cheek, he couldn't stop himself from closing his eyes and leaning in to her touch.

"I'm tired," he admitted.

"Then sleep." She took his hand, tugging him onto the bed. "Everything will look better after a good long rest."

"Promise?" he asked with a sad, strangled laugh.

"Considering our current situation, all bets and promises are off. All I can tell you with one-hundred-percent accuracy is that my bed is awfully warm and cozy. Assuming Mr. Bojangles makes room, there should be plenty of space for the three of us."

Thank you, he wanted to say. But he was too tired. His confessions had taken a costly emotional toll. She consistently brought out the best in him, but what could he offer her?

Chapter Thirteen

The next morning, Tiffany woke to bright sun streaming through her bedroom windows. As usual, her lower back throbbed, as did her feet, but the blissful warmth of being spooned against Rowdy overrode all complaints. He rested his big hand on her even bigger tummy and suddenly, for the first time since she couldn't remember when, all seemed right in her world.

But for how long?

Her growling stomach and the fact that she

had to pee provided excellent reasons to ignore the nagging question.

She eased from the bed without waking Rowdy—or Mr. Bojangles, who shared Rowdy's pillow—shoved her giant feet into cozy slippers, wrapped herself in her robe, then visited the bathroom before trudging down the stairs to find food.

Heavenly smells led her to the oven-warmed kitchen, where Pearl was already busy baking.

"It's about time." Pearl clanged her wooden spoon on the edge of a pot simmering with apple pie filling. The sweet-spicy smell of cinnamon and nutmeg and brown sugar made Tiffany even hungrier. Hands on her hips, Pearl said, "I don't have many rules around here, but as an unmarried, pregnant young woman, I would appreciate you not fornicating in my—"

"Grammy, promise, all Rowdy and I did was sleep." She gave her grandmother the abridged version of what had happened with Rowdy while he'd been overseas. "He was exhausted and needed a soft place to land. That's it."

"Now that he knows how precious life is, I'm assuming this adoption business has once and for all been taken off the table?"

"That's just it…" Tiffany took an iced Santa cookie from a plate on the counter. "He's more determined than ever to go through with the adoption. He basically said he can't quit his job. Because of that, he doesn't feel justified in raising a child only to potentially leave him."

Pearl scowled. "That's the biggest bunch of hogwash I've heard in all my days. Not a single one of us are given out guarantees along with our birth certificates. In this life, you get what hand you're dealt, and you deal with it. Period. Look what happened with you and your mom. I don't say this often, but I'm proud of the way you two have managed to carry on."

"Thank you." Tiffany bowed her head. Coming from her strong, proud grandmother, who had buried her husband and seen her only son imprisoned, the praise meant a lot.

"I think you and Rowdy ought to put this whole baby business aside—at least as long as you can. Enjoy the holidays and get to know each other the way a man and woman should. You two put your cart *waaaay* before the horse with your baby. How about slowing things down? Help me decorate cookies and then help your mom with her giant fancy tree. Try acting like a couple instead of already frazzled parents."

Misty-eyed at her grandmother's practical yet much-needed advice, Tiffany nodded.

"Never thought I'd get used to all this white stuff," Gigi said. She flounced into the kitchen wearing an emerald-green caftan with ostrich feathers and jewels around the neck. She already wore full makeup—including her false eyelashes. "But look at it shining in the sun.

Looks like an entire world filled with diamonds." She gave Tiffany a hug, then Pearl.

"What's got you so chipper this morning?" Pearl asked.

"It's almost Christmas, my very pregnant daughter is almost married and I have an afternoon call scheduled with Big Daddy. What more could a girl need?" She giggled.

"Indeed," Pearl said. "Although, this girl could use help with the dishes. Any volunteers?"

"I'll do it."

All three women turned to find Rowdy standing on the kitchen threshold. He wore faded Wranglers and a US Navy sweatshirt, and his short hair looked adorably mussed. Stubble lent him a bad-boy appeal. The way he cradled Mr. Bojangles made it entirely too easy for Tiffany to imagine him carrying their son. His good looks made it impossible to find her next words. His willingness to help her grand-mother only compounded his charm.

"You're a good man, Rowdy Jones." Pearl wiped her hands on her white apron. "After that, you and Tiffany eat a nice hearty break-fast. Then there's plenty more to do around here to get this old house decorated and spit shined for Christmas. Oh—and if you really want to get on my good side, the chickens need checking on, and the front and back walks need shoveling again."

"Yes, ma'am."

Two hours into his chore list, the man wasn't even winded.

Meanwhile, Tiffany's lower back was on fire and her feet felt like great big Christmas hams.

Mr. Bojangles, being the ultimate diva, snoozed on a sofa pillow in a patch of living room sun.

A fire crackled in the hearth, Dean Martin crooned carols and the air smelled heavenly from her grandmother's latest batch of gingerbread men.

Gigi sat at the dining room table, polishing heirloom silver Tiffany prayed wouldn't have to be sold.

"You made this?" In front of the fresh-cut tree a neighbor had delivered and settled into its stand not an hour earlier, Rowdy held up a pink salt-dough snowman ornament. After twenty years, crooked rhinestones and heavy-handed glitter still shone.

"Yes, I did." Afraid he might be poking fun at the treasured keepsake, she snatched it from him. "What about it? Think it's lame?"

"I like it." When Gigi wasn't looking, he stole a kiss hot enough to at least temporarily make her forget how bad she was hurting. "In fact, it's the cutest damned thing I've seen in a while—aside from its creator." The look in his eyes made her knees as unsteady as her feet. As it generally did whenever she was around him, her pulse went haywire. "I love learning more about you from happier times—assuming when you made this you were happy?"

Before nodding, she wiped away silly, sentimental tears. "I was a blessed child. Mom and Daddy spoiled me rotten—not just with material things but love and attention. When they couldn't be with me, I had nannies." While she added red velvet bows to the tree, her voice took on a wistful tone. "We traveled the world. London, Paris, Switzerland, Milan."

"What was your favorite?"

"The Alps. No contest."

"Interesting." He placed another homemade ornament front and center. A small-sized paper plate with horrible green paint, an obscene amount of glitter and an adorable, crooked photo of her with no front teeth. "I had you pegged for more of a Paris gal."

She shook her head. "Don't get me wrong, I love everything about Paris, but something about those mountain views…" The longing in her voice made him want to be the next man to show her that view. Impossible, since he'd return to duty as soon as the baby was born and safely transferred to Jeb's and Susie's capable arms.

Just thinking about that moment—handing over his son—made him physically ill. But if Rowdy intended to stay in the navy, it had to be done. The last thing he wanted was for his boy or Tiffany to wear the same grief-stricken look in their eyes as Duck's wife and sons. "Does your grandma have any antacid?"

"In the hall bathroom's medicine cabinet. Are you okay?"

"Yeah," he covered. "I just ate two more servings of Pearl's biscuits and gravy than I should have."

"I know the feeling." Her grin brightened his world. It was the same one from the ornament's picture. Sure, she now had all of her teeth and wore her hair swept up instead of in pigtails, but for an instant, her happy glow was back.

How could he make it stay after the adoption, after he'd gone?

By late that afternoon, even Tiffany was shocked by the progress they'd made. Fresh fir garlands had been hung from the stair railing—courtesy of another neighbor in exchange for six dozen of her grandmother's frosted cookie masterpieces. The tree was trimmed, and more garland hung from the mantel, as did cards from Pearl's many friends. Pearl punched holes in the corners of each one and hung them by ribbons from the garland and tree.

Her mother's Christmas village had come to life on the dining room buffet, and the nativity scene played out on the entry hall table.

Rowdy sat on the floor beneath the tree, putting together a train track. His focus made her smile from her perch on the sofa, where she assembled festive bags of candy for her grand-mother to gift to friends who stopped by.

For only a moment, Tiffany allowed herself the indulgence of imagining Rowdy and their son putting the train on its track together. It could be their annual thing—just the way when she was little, Big Daddy used to heft her high enough to put the angel on top of their tree.

"Hold your breath…" Rowdy flipped the on switch for the train's engine. "The *North Pole Express* will soon be chugging down the track."

Nothing happened.

Mr. Bojangles barked at the still train.

"Damn." Rowdy's little-boy expression of disappointment squeezed her heart. Her mind swirled with future possibilities for their son that would never come true. He opened the engine's bottom panel. "Got any AAA batteries?"

"I'll see…" The walk from the living room to the kitchen was a killer. Her lower back ached as if she'd spent her morning hauling hay bales as opposed to featherlight ornaments.

She returned with the batteries, then thankfully sank back onto the sofa cushions alongside her dog.

"All right." After replacing the batteries, Rowdy flipped the engine's switch. When it rhythmically chugged, he reattached it to the rest of the train. "Oh, yeah." His broad smile eased her pain. "Santa's gonna for sure visit your house. And when he does, you'll have me to thank." He winked before rising to join her and Mr. Bojangles. "This old house looks pretty damned good."

"Hey—I helped."

"Yes, you did. From the looks of your feet—too much." He eyed her swollen ankles. "You should have stopped working four hours ago."

"Probably, but then—" she lowered her

voice, nodding to Pearl, who stood in the dining room, tears glistening in her eyes "—we wouldn't have the pleasure of seeing my grandmother so happy."

"But she's crying," he said.

"Trust me, those are the good kind of tears. Clearly, you haven't been around enough women to know the difference."

Their gazes caught and locked. For the longest time, she forgot to breathe. Was he on the verge of kissing her again? Did she want him to?

No.

Maybe?

Yes.

Their physical chemistry made their rocky emotional connection all the more confusing. Just because he'd given her a second fabulous night between the sheets didn't mean squat. Not really. To marry him, to keep their son and make a family, they shouldn't have had sex but made love.

"Need a glass of water?" Rowdy asked. "You've got that blotchy-and-red look again."

"Thanks." She grimaced. Just what every girl longed to hear.

"You two have made me so happy." Pearl touched tree branches as if ensuring they were real. "The only thing that would make this Christmas brighter is if your father could be with us, but he'll come home soon enough. In the meantime, we have your wedding and the baby to look forward to."

"Grandma..." Tiffany forced a breath. "You know there's not going to be a wedding. Jeb and Susie will be raising our baby. It's for the best." After her and Rowdy's hot reunion, she'd thought the two of them as a couple— the three of them as a family—might actually make sense, but with the death of his friend, it seemed as if Rowdy's mind was as set on the adoption plan as hers had once been.

Pearl waved off Tiffany's comment. "Rowdy, I hate to trouble you after you've already put in such a long day, but could you please check the chickens' heating lamp? I took them some scraps and it's cold enough out there for my son's lawyers to put their hands in their own pockets."

"Yes, ma'am. I'll get right on it." To Tiffany he asked, "Need anything before I go? A cup of that herbal tea you like? A cookie or muffin?"

She shook her head.

Once he left, the lights on the tree seemed dimmer. The pine boughs didn't smell nearly as fresh. What was wrong with her? He'd been gone literally one minute, yet she missed him. She wasn't supposed to feel anything for him. But what if she did?

She pressed her hands to their baby. "Is it wrong for me to wish Rowdy had never come home?" Because if he hadn't, she wouldn't now be panic-stricken by the thought of him leaving again.

"I WAS BEGINNING to wonder when we'd next see the whites of your eyes." James sat astride his favorite paint, Charlie.

"Sorry." Rowdy rode Lucky on their way out to the southeast pasture, where a momma and her new calf needed checking. With a herd as big as theirs, it never failed that at least once during a winter storm, something would go wrong. "For the past few days, Tiffany's been complaining of her back hurting, so I've been taking care of her while doing odd jobs for her kooky mom and grandma."

"Those two are quite a pair," his dad chuckled. "Good folks, though. At the last church charity auction, Gigi brought in some fancy brand of shoes. The womenfolk damn near gave themselves aneurysms trying to outbid each other. Boy, was I relieved your mom didn't win."

Rowdy laughed, tipping the brim of his cowboy hat lower to cut the wind's icy licks at his cheeks.

For as far as he could see, the world was white.

The sky kissed the ground in an angry slash of gunmetal gray, promising more snow by morning. The very air smelled cold and forlorn. The horses exhaled deeply as they struggled through the snow.

"Your brother tells me you decided to go along with the adoption?"

"I s'pose."

"You're a grown man, so I guess it's none of my business, but for the record, this news didn't sit well."

Rowdy clamped his lips tight.

"You're breaking your momma's heart."

"What do you want me to say, Dad? I just

had a close friend die while clenching my hand. Know what the last thing he said was? He asked me to tell his wife and kids how much he loved them. Carl accused me of being selfish for giving my kid up for adoption. But you know what I think is even more selfish? Willingly bringing not just one child into this world but multiples, knowing the whole while that at any given time, you could be shot down and leave not just them but their mom. To me, that's unconscionable."

"Are you honestly that dense?"

"Excuse me?"

"Do you think you and your hotshot SEAL buddies own the patent on dying? Hell, son, I've had more than a few close calls in my day. For that matter, so has your mom—namely, while giving birth to you. In the end, all any of us are guaranteed is the here and now. Which means you need to embrace life by the cojones and live every day as if it may be your last.

I'm sorry your friend died, but do you think his wife or children regret having had him in their lives?"

For the rest of the ride, Rowdy remained silent.

Cold air seared his lungs.

It crept into his bones until every inch of his body ached.

By the time they'd returned to the barn, cared for the horses and headed for the house, light snow was already falling.

"Weatherman says this one's going to be a real dandy," his father said.

Rowdy merely grunted.

"Izzy and Ingrid have their school Christmas show tonight. Hope the storm holds off till they get done singing."

"I should probably go check on Tiffany."

"Why don't you bring her? You've been around the house so little your nieces aren't going to recognize you."

"I'm sure Carl and Justine wouldn't want us ruining the girls' big night."

"Nonsense." His dad patted his back. "Get washed up, then go grab your girl. Show starts at seven, but the gym gets awfully crowded, so you shouldn't be late."

"THIS ISN'T A good idea," Tiffany said once they'd made it down Pearl's front walk, which Rowdy had just shoveled.

Snow tumbled like clumps of white cotton candy.

The neighbors' Christmas lights lent the street a magical glow.

He pretty much lifted her onto the passenger seat of his truck, and the close contact made her treacherous body hum. Even worse, the baby kicked her ribs. The pain ricocheted through her, making her back hurt all the more. But then his stupid-handsome face was within kissing range and she forgot everything except how good it had felt when the two of them had finally come together. Desperate to think of anything but being with him again, she asked, "What if your mom and sister-in-law hate me?"

"Why would you care? Once you have the baby, aside from running into them at the grocery store, odds are that you won't see them again."

"Nice…" She shivered as he climbed in beside her.

"The only reason I'm even bringing you is because my dad gave me a guilt trip."

A wall formed at the back of her throat.

Was he deliberately trying to hurt her? Losing his friend had changed him. He'd lost his playful edge.

"I know that pouty look." He started the engine. Let it idle until warm air spilled from the heater vents. "Apparently, Mom wants to meet you—not that it will make a difference in how either of us feels, right? I mean, we're both still full speed ahead with the adoption?"

Darting her gaze away from him and out the fogging window, she nodded.

"Tonight is all about getting our point across. We need to make my family understand why we've decided on this mutually beneficial arrangement."

"What are you afraid of, Rowdy? And don't give me that line about you losing your friend. I understand that was rough on you, but what else changed?"

"Excuse me?" He pulled his truck into the already snow-packed street.

"Remember when you first blew back into town like a bull charging a rodeo clown? How you demanded to have custody of your son, and how you refused to even think about adoption?"

"Sure. But clearly, I was wrong." He'd reached

the stop sign at the end of the street. "Doesn't that make you happy?"

No.

The house on the corner had a giant inflatable Santa all lit up and waving in the gusty wind. The cheery sight made Tiffany sadder. Hugging her baby—their baby—she wished she knew when all of this had gone so horribly wrong. Before Rowdy came back to town, she'd been sure about the adoption, too. Now?

Nothing made sense. Especially not how much she'd grown to depend upon Rowdy for everything, from getting her tea and cookies to helping her in and out of cars. Just like every other man in her life, he'd soon be leaving. She had to not only accept that fact but make peace with it.

Besides, what she felt for Rowdy was purely physical. She didn't especially care for his stupid-handsome grin or the way his hair usually stuck out at crazy angles or how his Wranglers fit just right. She sure wasn't attracted to his goofy jokes or the way he was always accommodating and kind with her mom, grandmother and even Mr. Bojangles.

Considering all of those points, why did she care if he'd soon be leaving?

Good question.

One for which her aching heart had no answer.

Chapter Fourteen

What are you afraid of?

Through the entire awful holiday show, which included dancing candy canes, an evil elf and a pint-size Santa stuffed with so much padding that the poor kid could hardly walk, Rowdy pondered Tiffany's question.

He tried blaming his dour mood on the gymnasium's sweltering heat. Or how the lady in the seat next to him had been far too generous with her sticky-sweet perfume. He even hated the way his mom and Justine instantly sat Tiffany between them, coddling her like she was a rare and precious jewel.

Why did he resent them treating her like she was something special?

Because she was.

Only he was too big of a coward to step up and admit it. Damn right he was afraid. Not just of being a screwup as a dad, or dying, but of being equally as bad at this whole relationship thing he and Tiffany kept dancing around.

Stepping up?

Doing the so-called right thing by her and his child?

That would mean giving up the only way of life he knew. Sure, he could marry and still be a SEAL. Guys did it all the time. And they didn't die. But like his mom had long ago pointed out, a whole lot of them ended up divorced. Most had kids who lived full-time with their mothers. They saw them only on weekends or holidays—not nearly enough to make a real difference in their lives.

When the show finally ended and the entire family moved to the cafeteria for cake and punch and cookies, Rowdy stayed on the fringe, watching how naturally Tiffany interacted with his nieces. She wore one of the outfits he'd bought for her in Bismarck—a green sweater with the matching glitter shoes. The color made her eyes spark. He wanted her with a visceral pull. He wanted her away from all of these people to selfishly keep her to himself. But how did that desire fit in with his equally strong need to get out of Dodge?

Blaring Christmas carols combined with kids hyped up on sugar made his head scream for peace and quiet.

"She's pretty special," Justine said with a nudge to his arm. "Don't you dare think of letting her and your baby go."

"Mind your own business," he said in a gruff tone.

"Unfortunately, once I married your brother, that made you family, which makes you—and now Tiffany—very much my business. Not only is she gorgeous, but she's educated and funny and sweet. A real keeper."

He growled.

Rowdy escaped his sister-in-law to help himself to the syrupy-sweet punch. He would have gotten some for Tiffany, but his dad had already beaten him to it.

His mom caught up with him just as he filled a red Solo cup. "Don't think it hasn't escaped my notice that you're avoiding me."

"Mom…" He sighed.

"Tiffany's a lovely girl. She'll make a wonderful addition to our family."

Yeah, too bad it's not gonna happen.

"At first, when Tiffany's mother approached

me about a holiday wedding, I thought we might be jumping the gun, but now I think—"

"Drop it." The instant his gruff command sprang tears to his kindhearted mother's eyes, he regretted it. He reached out to hug her, but after a look of disgust, she spun on her heels and was gone.

What are you afraid of?

Tiffany's question raised its ugly head.

Hell, maybe he was afraid of everything? Not just of dying but of truly living.

Any time he'd taken a stab at even a brief relationship, it had ended in disaster. Why should this time be different?

Because Tiffany's different. Better. She makes you better.

He felt her gravitational pull as if she were the sun and he a lowly planet. A glance up had their gazes locked. When she shyly smiled and waved, resting her free hand on their baby, his chest tightened.

Despite the hundreds of people milling about the room, he had eyes only for her. What did that mean?

He raked his fingers through his hair, forcing himself to look away first. Out of all the missions he'd been on, Tiffany Lawson was by far the most dangerous.

If he allowed himself to fall for her, he feared losing the only life he'd ever known.

"PROMISE YOU'LL COME Saturday to help Justine and me make cranberry bread? Bring your mom and Pearl, too."

Tiffany nodded, then stepped into Rowdy's mother's latest hug. Had there ever been a sweeter, gentler woman? No. Which begged the question, how in the world had she created such a glowering son?

"It was great finally meeting you," Justine said. "We were beginning to think you were Rowdy's imaginary friend."

Tiffany laughed.

Isobel and Ingrid, still wearing their matching icicle costumes, danced around their mom.

"Miss Tiffany?" asked Isobel, the oldest girl, who sported longer strawberry blond hair and a constellation of adorable freckles.

"Yes?" Tiffany said.

"When my mom had Ingrid inside her, she said it was because Daddy gave her too much watermelon and she swallowed a seed and it growed inside her. Did Uncle Rowdy give you too much watermelon?"

Tiffany's cheeks superheated. "Something like that."

Justine covered her inquisitive daughter's ears. "Sorry. Seemed like the most reasonable explanation at the time."

"I understand," Tiffany said with a smile. What she didn't understand was why she hadn't met Rowdy's awesome family sooner. Was he ashamed of her? Those first days when he'd roared into town, he'd practically forced her to see his mom and try one of her home-made cinnamon rolls. But then he'd dropped the whole matter the way he had the idea of keeping their baby.

After more laughter and hugs and plenty of opportunities for Tiffany to see firsthand what amazing people had raised her baby's father, she grew all the more confused. Right now—through the baby she carried inside her—she shared a connection with these lovely people. They had to know about her plans for adoption, but there hadn't been any pressure from James or Patsy to keep their grandchild in the family.

Did they not care whether she and Rowdy kept the baby? Or did they care so much that they trusted them to make the right decision—whatever that might be?

After paying a dollar to retrieve her coat, hat and gloves from the Scouts, who'd made a fund-raiser out of their coat-check services, Rowdy led her outside.

The snow had stopped looking pretty and was now wind-driven pellets that stung when they hit her exposed cheeks.

"Get back inside," Rowdy said. "I'll go get the truck."

She usually would have argued, but in the past hour, the pain in her lower back had amped up to an alarming degree. Assuming it was from standing too long while chatting with Rowdy's family, she'd put the pain from her mind to enjoy the evening, but now the sharp stabs were growing harder to ignore.

Rowdy helped her to a bench in the school lobby, then said, "This time, please be here when I get back."

"Can't make any—" She winced.

"What's wrong?"

"Nothing." She shooed him away. "Just my back. I'm fine."

His gaze narrowed, but then he said, "If you do happen to need the facilities, leave your hat to let me know you're okay."

"Yes, sir." She'd intended to give him a sassy salute, but the latest round of pain hit sharp enough to make her gasp. She clutched her lower back.

"When did this start?"

"I don't know," she said through clenched teeth. "My back always hurts, but this—"

"Shit." He looked to her, then at the blowing snow. "To be safe, we should probably call 9-1-1, but with this storm, my gut's telling me I could probably get you to the hospital faster."

She shook her head. "I'll be fine. It's just those Braxton Hicks contractions my baby books talk about."

An hour later, while being prepped for an emergency C-section because of tests showing she'd suffered a placental abruption, Tiffany learned she couldn't have been more wrong.

She held out her hand to Rowdy. "I'm scared."

"Me, too. But everything's going to be okay." He kissed her forehead. She wanted him to kiss her lips. To claim her and their baby as his own.

Three nurses and two doctors bustled about her in the birthing room's cramped space. The fetal monitor reminded her with each rapid-fire beep that their son was in distress. He was a month premature, yet without the surgery, odds were he wouldn't survive at all.

Rowdy held her hand until she was being wheeled away from him and toward an operating room.

Terror didn't come close to describing her turbulent emotions.

Would her baby be okay?

Would she live to meet him?

Once she held him in her arms, would she ever have the strength to let him go?

"MR. JONES?" A NURSE hovered near the waiting room's entrance.

"Yeah. That's me." Startled, Rowdy glanced up from where he'd sat in the uncomfortable chair for the past hour. "How is the baby? And Tiffany? She okay?"

"They're both fine. Your son is small, but thankfully, his lungs are fully developed and at five pounds three ounces, he's a good size for being a month premature. As for his momma, she's good, too. But will be sore and sleepy for a while."

He nodded.

"I saw on your wife's birth plan that—"

"We're not married."

"I'm sorry. I just assumed…"

"It's okay."

"Well, since you're not together, I guess it makes sense that your baby is being adopted. I notified the adoptive parents of his safe delivery, but because of the storm, it may take them a while to get here. I thought you might like a few minutes alone with him?"

"Sure. Thanks." Rowdy swallowed hard.

Everything had happened so fast after his nieces' show that he hadn't called his parents or even Gigi or Pearl. All he'd been capable of focusing on was Tiffany and his son.

At 10:00 p.m. the nursery was quiet. The overhead lights had been dimmed. Two infant girls snoozed in clear plastic bassinets. Three nurses talked quietly at their station.

"Wash your hands." The nurse who had come to get him pointed toward a counter-mounted sink. "Then please put this on." She handed him a yellow paper gown. "When you're done, have a seat in the rocker, and I'll bring your son."

Rowdy forced a few deep breaths.

He wasn't sure what he'd expected, but this overwhelming panic wasn't it. What if he dropped the kid? What if he squeezed him too hard?

Finished with the nurse's instructions, he sat in the appointed chair, and she placed the impossibly small creature in his arms. It was then Rowdy realized his biggest problem—what if he fell in love?

Staring down at this tiny sleeping miracle, Rowdy found himself gaping in awe. This was his son.

His son.

For all these weeks, he'd fretted about the adoption issue, wavering back and forth. But in this most sacred moment, the decision had already been made. No matter what, he was keeping his child.

Period.

End of story.

He wiped tears with the sleeves of his gown, then inspected his little guy's perfect pink fingers. He was wrapped snug in his fuzzy blue blanket, so Rowdy figured there'd be plenty of time later to count his toes.

John Wayne Jones was already a looker.

And then he opened dazzling blue eyes. Rowdy knew lots of babies were born with blue eyes, but there was no denying an instant connection.

"Hey, buddy. You popped out early, but that's okay. Now that you're here, I'm never letting you go." In that instant, Rowdy knew why his brother called him selfish. But in his defense, before cradling his son in his arms, Rowdy had had no idea the lengths he'd go to fight for him. For Tiffany. For the family it only made sense for them to form.

He supposed he needed to run all of this past her, but proposing was a formality. Now that their son had entered their world, nothing else mattered besides making sure he had the best possible life.

Two hours passed before a nurse took him to the room to which Tiffany had been assigned.

"Hey, gorgeous." He presented her with a bundle of limp blue carnations he'd found for sale in the cafeteria. "How are you feeling?"

"Awful," she said with a faint smile. "How's the baby? Have you seen him?"

"He's spectacular. But with a mom and dad as good-looking as us, how could he be anything but gorgeous, right?"

"You're not getting attached, are you? The nurse told me Jeb and Susie are on their way. I can't—" Tears streamed down her cheeks. She looked away. "I don't think I can see him and still let him go."

"Babe…" He touched his fingers to her chin, urging her to look his way. "Our son's not going anywhere. Once you get your first look at him, I know you'll agree. He's the most perfect kid ever in the history of kids."

"Really?" Her voice quivered. "You think we should keep him?"

"There's nothing to think about. This is a no-brainer. The second I held him, I knew I was destined to be his dad. You're going to make a great mom. Together, we'll be the best parents any kid ever had."

"What about your career?"

"As soon as my current enlistment ends, I'll retire."

"Just like that?"

He snapped his fingers. "Just. Like. That."

Crying harder, she nodded and sniffled.

He kissed her, vowing to never again allow her lips to taste of salty tears. From here on out, he would do his best to make sure her life consisted of nothing but smiles.

"I want to see him," she said. "Hold him."

"I can make that happen." Rowdy pressed the nurse's call button.

Minutes later, the woman wheeled in their sleeping son and placed him in Tiffany's arms.

Once the nurse left them alone, Tiffany teared again, touching her pinkie finger to the tip of the infant's nose, to his chin, his suckling lips. "He is beautiful, isn't he?" Her voice held a note of awe. "I didn't dare let myself dream of a moment like this. I knew giving him up would be the hardest thing I'd ever done, but better for him, you know?"

"I get it. I thought the same. The whole adoption plan made so much sense—it was the *only* thing that made sense. But then I saw him and..." She wasn't the only one who'd gone soft. For a guy who was supposedly a big strong SEAL, Rowdy had turned into a gentle giant.

"What are we going to tell Susie and Jeb?" she asked in a whisper. "They'll be devastated."

"Sorry, but we can't give them our child to save hurt feelings."

She sniffled but nodded.

Outside big picture windows, snow fell harder, frosting the world in white. Deep satisfaction settled over Rowdy. Though he felt physically exhausted, he was on such an emotional high that he doubted he'd ever be able to sleep.

"What should we name him?" Tiffany asked.

"Is there any doubt?"

"No…" She shook her head.

"Oh, yes. While you were still out of it, I already christened him John Wayne Jones."

"Absolutely not."

"Yes." He leaned over her bed rail, kissing her forehead.

"No."

Her cheeks.

"No."

Her nose.

"Rowdy…"

Finally, her lips.

When she sighed, then groaned, opening her mouth to the sweep of his tongue, he knew he'd gotten his way. As for whether or not the rest of their lives would go as planned, only time would tell.

Chapter Fifteen

"We got here as soon as we— Oh." Susie froze before fully entering Tiffany's room.

The moment Tiffany had been dreading ever since she and Rowdy made their late-night decision to keep their son had arrived.

Susie paled, then clung to her husband.

Tiffany tugged the receiving blanket higher over her left breast, from which she'd been trying to get Johnny to suckle. The connection was painfully clear. If Tiffany and Rowdy had planned on going through with the adoption, she wouldn't now have been breast-feeding her son.

"I'm sorry," Tiffany said. The words felt woefully inadequate in light of the gift she'd rescinded. "I promise to pay back every dime you've spent on my medical care."

"It's not the money," Susie said. "This has never been about that. If we could just buy a baby, don't you think we would have?" Tears streamed down her cheeks, dredging a deep crevasse through Tiffany's heart. "I knew this would happen. All along, this has been my biggest fear. Why couldn't you have told us sooner? Why did you have to string us along?"

"Because she honestly didn't know." Rowdy entered the room behind them. He carried the lime Jell-O she'd craved from the cafeteria, as well as a coffee for himself. "If you need a punching bag, use me. This was one of those things we never saw coming."

"I don't believe that for a second," Susie said.

Her low tone was angry enough that it might as well have been a scream. "The day you entered the picture, everything changed."

"Let's go." Jeb turned his wife toward the door. The consummate politician, he bowed his head. "Tiffany, Rowdy, we wish you well."

They were gone, but Tiffany couldn't stop shivering.

"Need me to turn up the heat?" Rowdy asked.

She shook her head. "That whole exchange left me feeling cold on the inside. Like I've made a horrible mistake in hurting Susie and Jeb so deeply."

"What about you? Me? Our son? Don't our feelings matter?"

"Of course. But I made them a promise I couldn't keep. Maybe I was wrong in ever thinking I could?"

"It doesn't matter." He slipped his arm around her shoulders. "I feel for what Jeb and Susie must be going through, but hon, this wasn't just your decision. They'll grieve for a while, but hopefully, find another child. I'm sure they don't blame you."

"You make it sound so simple. So black-and-white."

"It is."

"It's not, Rowdy. This whole situation is a thousand murky shades of gray. You and I don't know the first thing about being parents or a couple. What if we're making a mistake?"

Baby Johnny whimpered at her breast.

Her milk hadn't yet come in, and even if it had, it didn't feel as if Johnny had latched on properly to her nipple—not like her books said he was supposed to. Where was the euphoria new mothers supposedly felt when feeding?

Johnny's whimper grew into a full-blown cry.

She tried jiggling him and humming, but that only made his face turn screaming-baby red.

"Could you please take him?" She swaddled

her son, then drew her hospital gown over her breast.

"Of course." Rowdy cradled the infant to his chest, but that didn't help, either.

"Should we call the nurse?" Tiffany asked.

"Yes. I'm sure she'll have a trick up her sleeve that'll make him smile."

She didn't.

Rowdy called both of their families.

By midmorning, grandmothers appeared in full force, cooing and rocking and singing, but no matter how much comfort any of them gave, Johnny remained fussy. Even in his sleep, he appeared restless.

"When your milk comes in," Pearl said two days after his birth, "he'll calm right down. Seen it a hundred times with babies at the church nursery."

"He's got gas," Patsy said three days after his birth.

Almost four days after his birth, Justine said,

"I just read an article that said he might be missing the safety of your womb."

Tiffany struggled not to frown. Even if her son did miss his former cocoon, what was she supposed to do about it?

She envied all the moms pictured in the bucolic scenes in her parenting books. They sat up in their freshly made beds with their hair and makeup perfect while holding court, everyone congratulating them on their sweet-tempered babies.

Tiffany's surgical incision wasn't healing as expected, so her obstetrician opted to keep her a fifth day and night in the hospital. The more she thought about the mounting medical bill, the more panicked she grew, which in turn seemed to make her son all the more agitated.

The fact that she couldn't even manage to feed him, let alone nurture and soothe him the way a mother should, made her feel like a failure in every facet of her life.

Then there was Rowdy.

He helped as much as he could, but aside from bottle feedings, there wasn't much to be done. He haunted the cramped room's perimeters, most often standing with arms folded, a grim set to his mouth.

Once his mother and Justine and Pearl and Gigi left for the day and Tiffany and Rowdy were alone with their son, who finally slept, she summoned the courage to ask, "Do you ever regret keeping Johnny?"

The room was too dark for her to see him clearly, but his heavy sigh was unmistakable.

"Should I take that as a yes?"

"It's more complicated than that." He left the bench seat by the window to cautiously approach the bed. Afraid of waking their son? "I'd be lying if I said I hadn't had doubts, but my issues are more long-term. I'm already worrying about how to pay for college if I quit the navy. Logically, he'll grow out of this cranky stage, right?"

"I guess?" She managed a faint laugh. "When he's crying, do you ever feel panic? Like if he doesn't stop, you'll lose what little's left of your sanity?"

"Absolutely." As if relieved to not be alone on that count, he released a rush of air. "Another thing bugging the hell out of me? Our hovering families—always giving advice. If they're all such experts, then how come none of the crap they say to do actually works?"

"Excellent point."

They both fell silent.

Aside from the faint sound of a doctor being paged over the hall intercom, all in their world was blissfully silent, making Tiffany believe maybe everything would be okay.

If only Rowdy would step closer.

Take her hand.

Hug her or kiss her or reassure her he was in

this for the long haul, she might even believe he cared for her as a woman instead of just as the mother of his son.

Rowdy cleared his throat, then pointed at the general vicinity of her chest. "I, ah, don't mean to be staring at your boobs, but…"

After a flustered moment of embarrassment over his bizarre statement, she glanced down to find twin wet spots on her gown. She'd been so consumed by a multitude of worries that she hadn't noticed the new sensation of achy fullness in her breasts or the slight tingling to her nipples.

"Think your milk finally came in?"

"Yes. What should I do? Wake Johnny to see if he's ready to eat?"

"No," Rowdy said with a firm shake of his head. "One bit of advice my brother gave is to never under any circumstance wake a sleeping baby."

"Sounds wise." Tiffany grinned. For the first

time since Johnny's birth, she felt a glimmer of hope that she and Rowdy might actually survive their son's infancy—at least physically.

As for the two of them as a couple?

It was too soon to tell.

TWO DAYS BEFORE CHRISTMAS, while Rowdy sat on the chaise in Tiffany's room, watching her breast-feed their son, he realized the sight never got old. What did?

Gigi's blaring Sinatra holiday CD.

Pearl's never-ending parade of friends and cookie clientele all clamoring to see and hold the baby.

Most annoying of all? Tiffany's general vibe.

He was all the time catching her in a stare. He got the oddest sense she wanted—even expected—something from him, but what?

Finally, after their son had a turn on each breast, Rowdy came right out and asked, "Did I do something to piss you off?"

"No. Why?" Since having the baby, she'd lost her feisty edge. He used to love their epic bickering matches. The way her cheeks flushed when she was good and mad. How many times had he craved kissing the anger right out of her? Now he couldn't get a feel for what was even appropriate when it came to touching her. She always, always held Johnny in her arms.

Poor Mr. Bojangles sulked at the foot of the bed. He'd worn the same purple sweater for three days.

"Babe," Rowdy said, "you've changed."

"Of course I have. I'm a mother. Are you faulting me for caring for our son?" She touched her free hand to her messy ponytail.

"How long has it been since you put the baby down long enough to have a shower?"

"I don't know. Why? Do I smell?"

"No. And you're totally missing my point. What are we doing? How long are we going to stay with your mom and grandmother when we should be setting up our own house?"

"Is that what you want to do?"

"I thought it was understood?" Along with the fact that they'd get married and, as soon as she was medically able, resume bedroom activities that had nothing to do with their son and everything to do with exploring every inch of Tiffany's beautifully curvy body.

"How could any of that be understood when I can't remember the last time you touched me? Let alone kissed me?"

"Is that what you want? A kiss?"

"No." A strangled half laugh escaped her like a gas bubble. "That's the last thing I want from you. What would be great? Is you running to the store before it closes. We're almost out of diapers."

"Why don't you come with me? Leave the baby with Pearl and Gigi. Might do you good to get out of the house. The Christmas lights around the square are gorgeous with all the snow." *We could pretend we were on a date. Everything between us has been backward as hell. Most couples get to know each other before having a baby. But we...*

Hell, he couldn't finish his own thought. What he and Tiffany had become was untenable. The two of them weren't working on any level. But how did he fix a relationship that had never officially formed? Let alone been broken?

Gigi and Pearl maintained a firm stance on Rowdy not spending the night with her and the baby until they were married.

If Tiffany had a quarter for every time she'd told her mother a wedding wasn't happening, she'd wipe out all family debt and still have enough for new shoes.

It was now 3:00 a.m., Johnny suckled her breast and she'd be lying if she said she didn't miss her son's father. She had flat-out lied when she'd told him she didn't want him to kiss her or hold her or assure her everything would one day be all right. More than anything, she longed for the two of them to find a cozy home of their own. She wanted to fall asleep with him at night and wake up next to him each morning.

Did she love him?

She didn't know.

All she did know was that life was better with him in it. The time he'd been gone had proven that. But lately she'd noticed he wasn't as quick with his smiles. He didn't carry his shoulders as straight, and gone was his usual confident stride.

Since they no longer talked like they used to when he'd first come to town, she could only guess at the meaning behind his funk. The only logical conclusion was that he regretted his hasty decision to keep Johnny. To stay with her.

"I love you," she whispered to her son, smoothing the tip of her pinkie across his soft cheek. "Keeping you was the best decision of my life—even if we don't end up keeping your dad."

The last thing she'd want was for Rowdy to feel trapped.

Even more than she feared him leaving her, she feared him staying for all the wrong reasons, then growing to resent her and Johnny for taking him from the life he loved.

She could handle being a navy wife.

She could handle spending a large chunk of her life raising their son on her own. What she couldn't do was know Rowdy was with her only out of a sense of obligation. Because his family expected him to do the right thing.

If there was anything she'd learned during this experience, it was that there was no singular correct path in life. Every person had to make his or her own way. His or her own decisions. If Rowdy chose not to be with her and Johnny, so be it.

She had too much pride to beg him to stay.

Once Johnny had eaten his fill, she changed his diaper, then tucked him back into the crib that Rowdy had purchased and assembled next to her chaise.

"Come here," she said to Mr. Bojangles, who stared forlornly at her from the foot of the bed. "I'm sorry I haven't been giving you as much attention."

She snatched him up for a cuddle, then exchanged his purple sweater for pink-and-black zebra stripes.

He licked her in appreciation.

"I love you," she said. "You're the most loyal man I've ever had in my life."

He fell asleep in her arms.

She kissed the top of his furry head, then

turned out the light and settled for cuddling her dog rather than the big lug who apparently didn't want to be with her and his son enough to risk raising Pearl's and Gigi's hackles.

After a fitful night's sleep, Tiffany yawned her way to the hall bath, then used the time before Johnny woke to grab a quick shower.

Rowdy usually arrived at the house no later than eight. He helped with the chickens, then shoveled the front and back walks if there'd been any overnight snow.

But when she finished her shower, dressed and even towel-dried her hair and he still hadn't shown up, she forced a few deep breaths to fend off a full-blown panic.

What would she do if one day Rowdy just didn't come?

He'd already mentioned that after New Year's he was expected back on base, but until then, there was nothing binding him to her and Johnny. She looked in her vanity mirror. At the dark shadows beneath her bloodshot eyes and the extra weight she carried in her cheeks. She hadn't done her hair since their son's birth, and couldn't even find her makeup amid all of Johnny's baby gear.

She was mired so deep in more reasons why Rowdy no longer seemed attracted to her that when her cell rang, she jumped.

"Hey, sugar." Patsy's cheery tone felt out of tune with Tiffany's gloomy mood. Plus, the jazzy ringtone woke the baby.

"Hey. What's up?" She set her phone on the vanity, put the call on speaker, then lifted Johnny from his crib and into her arms.

Mr. Bojangles, still beneath the covers, stretched and yawned, poking just his head out into the chilly room.

"Uh-oh," Patsy said. "Did an angel wake up on the wrong side of his crib?"

"Not at all." Tiffany cradled him close and he quieted. "He's as sweet as Pearl's apple pie."

"Aw, I miss him. Which is part of the reason I called. First, Rowdy asked me to tell you he won't be by till later. His daddy's got a sick calf, and the only medicine is at a veterinary clinic two hours north. He and Carl volunteered to drive up to get it."

"Of course. I understand." But she didn't. Oh—she would never fault Rowdy for needing to help his family, but it might have been nice to pack up the baby and tag along. Since the girls were in school, Justine could have come, too. Like a double date. But since she and Rowdy weren't a couple, that probably wouldn't work.

"The second reason for my call is that I wanted to invite you, your mom and Pearl over for Christmas Eve. We'll have dinner and sing carols. It'll be fun. I figured for Johnny's first Christmas, we'd do it up real nice."

"Thank you." Tiffany blinked back tears.

"That sounds wonderful. What can I do to help? Do you need me to bring anything?"

"Nope. You've got your hands full with Johnny. Plus, I told Rowdy to watch the baby for you all afternoon so you'd have time for a nice soak in the tub and to doll yourself up for pictures."

"You're an angel for thinking of me." Her heart ached that Rowdy's mother had to nudge him to be kind. What had happened between them? Where had she gone wrong?

"My pleasure. Oh—and every year we take family pictures wearing matching sweaters. This year's color is white, so I'll send Rowdy with one for each of you."

"That's not—"

"Don't say another word. I already bought them and can't wait to see how Johnny looks. He'll be like a real live angel."

"Yes, ma'am, he will." Tiffany wished she were close enough to Rowdy's mom to ask her opinion on the awkwardness between them, but she wasn't. The last thing she wanted was for Patsy to find her pushy or demanding.

After a few more minutes' small talk, Tiffany said goodbye, then got on with her day. Whether Rowdy showed up or not, she still had a long morning and afternoon planned of feeding and doing laundry and helping Gigi and Pearl with their myriad of holiday preparations.

Sitting in her room moping wouldn't get anything done.

The sooner she got used to being a single mom, the better off she'd be.

"Sorry," Rowdy said to Tiffany when he didn't get to Pearl's house until after six that night.

She paced the living room, carrying their screaming, red-faced son in her arms.

Mr. Bojangles sat on the sofa high atop a

mountain of pint-size clothes waiting to be folded.

When Tiffany didn't look in his direction, Rowdy added above the wails, "We ended up driving clear to Benson County. Then Dad called and said our family vet had the medicine after all. We drove home, then Mom needed me to run a half-dozen errands for her party— she called you, right?"

Tiffany nodded, then gave the baby a jiggle.

Rowdy tweaked the little guy's sock-covered foot. "Want me to take him?"

She shook her head and kept right on walking.

"I assume you agreed to come—to Mom's party?"

She nodded.

"Thanks. Mom's excited to show off the baby."

"I'll bet."

"Where are Gigi and Pearl?"

"Their garden club is having a holiday dinner at the Sizzler."

"Why didn't you go?"

"Maybe because I'm not a member?"

"What's with the attitude?"

"Gee, could it be because I've been trying to calm our son for the past six hours?"

"Sorry. I never thought all the crap I had to do would take so long."

"It's okay."

"No, it's not. We're in this together, and I want to help." Rowdy settled his hands around Johnny's waist, taking their son. He held him extra close, cupping his hand to the back of Johnny's head. His screams faded to whimpers.

"I hate you." Tiffany collapsed on the sofa with enough force to startle Mr. Bojangles into a barking frenzy, which in turn made Johnny cry. She said to the dog, "Now I hate you, too."

Rowdy soon enough calmed the baby again. "Look, I'm sorry I haven't been here for you today."

"I'm sorry I snapped. Johnny's crying spells make me feel helpless. It's the worst."

She sighed, running her fingers through her messy hair. She looked nothing like the woman he'd slept with last Easter, but she was still every bit as beautiful to him. There was so much he wanted to say, but how did he start? First, he wanted things to change between them—to get better.

He cleared his throat. "You know how I have to be back on base after New Year's?"

She nodded.

"Which would be easier for you? Tagging along with me? Or staying here? You'd have Pearl and Gigi to help. Plus my mom and Justine. I'd miss you something fierce for the eighteen months left on my enlistment, but am I being selfish in wanting you two with me? If you stay, I guess logistically, it makes more sense. To save money, you and Johnny could still live with Pearl and Gigi. What do you think?"

Her gaze shone with tears, but not a single one fell.

She stood, scooped up the dog, then said, "I'm taking a bubble bath. Thank you for watching Johnny until I'm done."

Sounds fun. Mind if I join you?

Rowdy squashed his inner horndog. "What about my question? If you are going with me, I'll need to start making plans—unless you wouldn't mind bunking with a few other smelly SEALs?"

She didn't laugh at his joke. In fact, she didn't even pause on her way to the stairs.

What did that mean? What was she thinking? Why wouldn't she talk to him? He was good at a lot of things, but mind reading had never been one of them.

He asked the baby, "Has she been salty all day?"

Rowdy studied the little guy's face. It was crazy how much he'd missed him. Rowdy had been pissed about the wild-goose chase his father had sent him on. It had taken precious time he would have otherwise spent with his son.

And Tiffany...

He sucked in a deep breath.

What did she want from him? What did she need?

The water went on upstairs.

Eyes closed, he thought about her all soap slick and sexy. Lately, she was impossible to read. He couldn't tell if she wanted him closer or to stay the hell away. Who knew, maybe if he went to Virginia without her, the separation might do them good?

The pang in his heart didn't agree.

Chapter Sixteen

"Rowdy, you shouldn't have." *But I'm sure glad you did.* Tiffany's heart swelled with unexpected, much-appreciated joy. It was Christmas Eve and the size and impressive wrapping job on the gift he'd just presented had to be significant.

Pearl and Gigi had long ago left the house to attend an early church service. They'd taken Johnny with them to show him off to their few friends who hadn't already seen him. Meaning she and Rowdy were finally alone.

To talk.

Hold hands.

Kiss.

Her gaze momentarily locked with his. Her cheeks flushed.

For the first time since she couldn't remember when, she'd had time to curl her long hair and apply makeup and even eyelashes. She'd done her nails and even added a spritz of her favorite floral perfume. Despite the fact that she currently wore her pink bathrobe and slippers, she felt beautiful under his stare.

"I didn't." Still standing in the entry hall, he cleared his throat, then shoved his hands in his jeans pockets.

Mr. Bojangles danced at his feet. She'd dressed him in a Santa suit for the occasion, but he'd already worked off his hat.

"Excuse me?" she asked on her way to the living room sofa. The square box was much too big for her to open while standing. The silver foil paper was embossed with elegant wreathes. Wide white ribbon had been tied into a giant bow.

"You thanked me for giving you the gift, but it's not from me but Mom." He cleared his throat. "I guess she told you about the family sweater thing she puts us through every year?"

"Yes." Her spirit sagged like one of those blow-up lawn ornaments after the holiday season. She should have guessed he didn't care enough about her to give her a gift.

"Don't get too excited. I'm sure it's just your sweater."

"Right. Thanks." She set the unopened box on the sofa beside her. Was now the time to give him her gift? And that other *thing*. She'd planned to wait until closer to his leaving, but she supposed now was as good a time as any. Like ripping a bandage off fast. The pain would be momentarily intense but then gone.

He'd wandered toward the Christmas tree,

still holding his hands in his pockets. "Tiff? Can we—"

"Wait here. I'll be right back." She couldn't bear one more second of awkward silence. Whatever magic the two of them had once shared was gone. She needed to get used to that fact.

In her room, she took a legal-sized envelope from her top dresser drawer, as well as a wrapped rectangular package.

Back downstairs, she found him still in front of the tree, head bowed. What was he thinking? Was he as sad about how things had ended between them as she was? The night of Johnny's birth, she'd been convinced the two of them might actually have a bright future, but now? She'd lost hope.

"I got you this." She gave him the box. "It's not much. But I…" She stopped before her raspy voice told her most tightly held secret. That during the time they'd spent together, she'd grown helplessly, ridiculously attracted to not only his stupid-handsome face but the way he so willingly gave of his time to her, Pearl and Gigi. The one thing he didn't seem capable of giving was his heart. But could she blame him? They might have shared a child, but they hadn't shared much else beyond chemistry. She'd been willing to try. But…

"Thanks. I, ah, got you a little something, but it's back at my parents' house."

"It's okay. Besides, the gift really is something small."

He tore off the paper and bow, setting them on the coffee table before opening the box. It held one of her favorite silver frames from her namesake store, Tiffany. It had been a gift to her from her father on her eighteenth birthday. She didn't currently have the money for a new frame but figured this would be infinitely more special. She'd positioned Johnny for an hour to get the perfect pose of him seated under the tree. He'd worn a red onesie. She'd tied a green bow around his waist, then propped him among the prettily wrapped, mostly home-made presents she and Gigi and Pearl would exchange.

"Tiff…" Tears welled in Rowdy's grassy-green eyes. "This is the best gift I ever could have gotten. Thank you. Seriously. He's everything to me."

But not me?

"There's a smaller, laminated photo, too. I thought you might want to keep it with you when you're deployed." Her throat ached while handing over the second part of her gift. "I called in a favor from Daddy's legal team and got them to work this up."

"What is it?" He gave the envelope a funny look, then seemed hesitant to open it, as if it were a prank and worms might fall out.

"Just a formality. Since you're leaving, I wanted there to never be a question regarding the fact that you're Johnny's father, but I thought there should at least be a few guidelines in place."

"Huh?" Brows furrowed, he asked, "Are these custody papers?"

"Yes. Just sign in a few places, and you'll be free to do whatever you want without worrying about Johnny."

"Come again?" He still looked confused.

"Give them a read when you can. The document basically states that I have full legal custody of our son but that you have my blessing to visit him as often as your schedule allows. Oh—and that—"

"Are you shitting me?" For a second, she thought he might explode, but then he regained his composure. "The fact that you would sink to this level of distrust when our boy is barely over a week old is..." He shook his head, clamped his lips tight. "I can't even begin to put words to what you've done. Get dressed.

Let's get my mother's party behind us—then you and I are going to launch the next world war, because, babe, there's no way in hell I'm signing over custody of my son. I'll be waiting in the truck."

What had she done?

While Rowdy exited the house, filling the entry hall with cold night air, Tiffany wished she'd handled this whole thing differently. Why hadn't she come right out and told him she wanted nothing more than to marry him and try giving their little family a chance at a happy ending?

The answer to that question was heartbreakingly simple. She couldn't tell him what she wanted, because she was afraid.

It was bad enough that he was leaving her, but if she handed him the extra rounds of emotional ammunition stemming from her admission? Well, that would be too painful to bear.

For Patsy's sake, she had to paste on a smile and somehow get through this awful night.

Later she and Rowdy could make their final goodbye.

Tiffany opened the oversize gift box, hands trembling from the fight.

The spellbinding beauty of what she found nestled amid silver tissue paper only made her feel worse. A white cashmere sweater with a Peter Pan collar dotted with shimmering crystals and pearls. The garment's opulence took her breath away. Tucked beneath it was a full floor-length white satin skirt with layers of tulle beneath. This was an outfit suitable for a Christmas bride…

No…

Gigi and Patsy and Pearl wouldn't dare?

But when Tiffany added up all of the instances of her grandmother and mother being oddly away from the house and how Rowdy's mom had been running him ragged with either errands or what could have been diversionary goose chases, it all made perfect sense.

What had Gigi and Patsy been thinking?

Obviously, Tiffany and Rowdy were in no shape to get married—they might never be. If her mother thought she could force the issue by literally forcing a wedding, she had another thing coming.

The next time Tiffany married would be the *last* time.

Her broken marriage had been beyond painful and she would never put herself—and now her son—through that again.

Even if Rowdy bowed to pressure and agreed to the ceremony, what then? What good could come of being tied to a man who clearly despised her?

Leaving the outfit in its box, Tiffany marched to the front door, tossed it open, then charged across the front porch and down the steps, where she promptly slipped on an icy patch and fell on her behind.

The pain was considerable, but she knew she'd live.

The shame of walking in on a surprise wedding with a groom who didn't want to be there—now, that would hurt!

"Tiff, what the hell?" Rowdy hopped from his truck to help. "Are you okay?"

"I'm fine. Not that you'd care!"

"What are you talking about? You're the one passing out custody papers like Christmas candy!"

"What else could I do? It's obvious you don't want to be with me."

"Are you mental? How many times have I told you we should be together?"

"We *should* be? I've already had one broken marriage, Rowdy. Now that I have a son to watch after, why in the world would I turn around and hitch my wagon to a man who doesn't even want me? Let alone love me?"

"Woman, now I know you've lost a few brain cells from lack of sleep. Those are your insecurities talking, because when I tell a woman I love her and want to marry her, I mean it."

"But you never said any of that!" she shrieked.

Inside the house, Mr. Bojangles barked.

A light snow began to fall.

"Great." She threw her hands up. "Now my makeup and hair will be ruined. I'm sick of snow!" she shouted to the heavens.

Rowdy knelt, taking her hands to help her to her feet.

He took the liberty of brushing snow from her behind, and she'd be lying if she said his lightest touch wasn't a thrill.

"Let me be real clear." He cupped her cheeks with his hands. "I adore you. I love you. I need you. When I leave for Virginia, more than anything, I want you and Johnny with me. I selfishly want you two seeing me off on every mission, and I want you waiting for me at the base for a kiss the second I get home. You're stubborn and sassy and will probably be the death of me, but until then, I'm never letting you go. How's that for plain talk? Unless you love plaid. If you do, then I'm gone." His hopeful wink told her he remembered their silly conversation on the topic while house hunting.

Was it possible he'd wanted her to be his future wife even back then?

Since the lump in her throat was too big to speak, she nodded and then kissed him so very hard. "Not only do I vow to never buy a plaid sofa, but I love you, too," she admitted when coming up for air. "I was so afraid—of everything. Of becoming a mom and wife and of needing you but you not needing me. Johnny needs his father and I need my man. God help me, but that man is you, Rowdy Jones."

"Damn straight. And don't ever forget it."

He wrapped his arms around her, hugging her right off the ground. He pressed his lips to her so softly, so sweetly, if she hadn't been so darned cold, she might have thought she was dreaming. "Want me to make a fire and we'll skip Mom's party?"

"The party—how could I forget what I raced out here to tell you? It's a setup."

"What do you mean?"

She explained her theory, topping it off by describing Patsy's over-the-top gift that wasn't exactly suitable for a family night of a casual dinner and carols.

"You know—" Rowdy scratched his head, then led her inside out of the cold "—that makes a lot of sense. I even tried calling my friend Logan yesterday, but he blew me off. Sounded like he was at an airport. Could he have been headed here?"

"Only one way to find out." She winked.

"But first, wanna have a little fun with our matchmaking mothers and grandmother?"

"You know it. But only if I get to help you dress." His slow and sexy wink was back, along with his stupid-handsome grin. He had enough dark stubble to make him look just like the bad-boy cowboy she'd instantly fallen for all those months ago.

On her tiptoes for one more kiss, she whispered, "I think that could be arranged."

Epilogue

Rowdy held Johnny while Tiffany ducked into the bathroom located just off the baggage-claim area at Norfolk International Airport. She was expecting again—this time, a girl. At eight months and three weeks, she was big as a house and prettier than ever. Also sassier than ever, but since their Christmas Eve wedding, he'd had plenty of time to figure out not only her many moods but what flavor of ice cream best soothed them.

"Any sign of our families?" Tiffany asked on

her way back to him with an impatient glance toward the passenger entrance.

"Not yet. Relax. Pearl will be fine."

"I know. But this is her first time in a plane. I want everything to be perfect."

"Since your dad got his early release for good behavior and sprang for them all to fly first class, I'm sure she's fine."

Big Daddy's release had come just in time for Valentine's Day. Gigi had been over the moon. An old college buddy back in Dallas had gotten him on board with a new high-paying position, and he and Gigi were back to living their old luxe life. Pearl's second mortgage had been paid in full, and all of that good news was enough to have had the two most important women in her life forgive them for faking a big fight, then calling off the surprise wedding.

After they'd assured their shocked guests and family that the quarrel was a joke, everyone had shared a good laugh and gotten on with the romantic event. Patsy had even arranged for a few of Rowdy's friends and their wives to be there—including Macy, Jessie and Hattie, who had become Tiffany's rocks whenever Rowdy was deployed.

Hattie owned a favorite SEAL hangout and had introduced Tiffany to loads more wives, who formed the best support system she could have wanted—although, she was still awfully excited to see her grandmother and mom.

"There they are." Rowdy pointed to the women accompanied by Tiffany's barrel-chested dad.

Tiffany's eyes welled and as best as she could, she waddled that way for a round of hugs.

Then came the baby cooing…

"Look at Johnny!"

"He's so big!"

"How cute!"

Then complaining...

"I didn't think we'd ever get here," Gigi said.

"Tell me about it." Patsy blew her nose from a tissue she'd taken from her purse. "Pearl and I have been on a plane since Bismarck. You two only had to fly from Dallas."

"True." Gigi smiled. "Maybe next time you'll listen when I invite you to stay with us for a few days before your Norfolk flight?"

On the walk out to the car, Tiffany's dad held her back. "Before we're all settled in for baby watch, I wanted to tell you how proud I am of the woman you've become. You're an amazing mother and wife and real estate agent—the total package. I love you."

"I love you, too, Dad." She stopped for a hug. "When you went away and then Crawford left me, there was a time when I never thought I'd love again. But then Rowdy came along, and..." she grinned "...now I've never been happier."

TWO MONTHS LATER, on a Saturday afternoon, Tiffany was breast-feeding Mariah in the ugly yet criminally comfy plaid recliner Rowdy had talked her into buying, when her cell rang. As was usually the case when she was busy with one of the kids, her phone was across the room.

"Rowdy!" she called.

"Got it!" He'd been changing Johnny's diaper but scooped up her cell on his way back into the living room and handed it to her.

"Hello?" she answered without looking at the caller.

"Tiffany?"

The woman sounded all too familiar.

"Susie?" Tiffany straightened with surprise. "H-how are you?"

"Actually, I'm the proud new mother of Cambodian twins. They're only eleven months old, but I can already tell they'll be geniuses."

"Of course they will." Residual pregnancy hormones brought on tears. "I'm so happy for you and Jeb." And she really, truly was. She'd felt awful about the way she'd ended her arrangement with the couple, but it couldn't have been helped. From the moment she'd laid eyes on him, she'd loved her son. Oh, who was she kidding? From the first beat of his heart, she'd been a goner.

Rowdy waved to get her attention. He whispered, "Everything okay?"

Perfect. Seriously, dazzlingly perfect.

While Susie chattered about her precious miracles, Tiffany blew Rowdy a kiss. After all of her years spent living in Dallas, she'd always assumed she'd end up with a Texas cowboy. Never in her wildest dreams would she have thought she'd get hitched to a navy SEAL cowboy from North Dakota.

But she wasn't complaining…

* * * * *